Why is it important to know about future things?

howdo grown-ups help me know and love Jesus?

What can I change to make me a nicer person?

D1505778

**To**

From

Date

# PAUL

## *Hits the Beach*
### *And Other Wild Adventures*

# PAUL

JILL & STUART BRISCOE
*pictures and cartoons by* **RUSS FLINT**
*music by* **LARRY MOORE**

Baker Books
A Division of Baker Book House Co
Grand Rapids, Michigan 49516

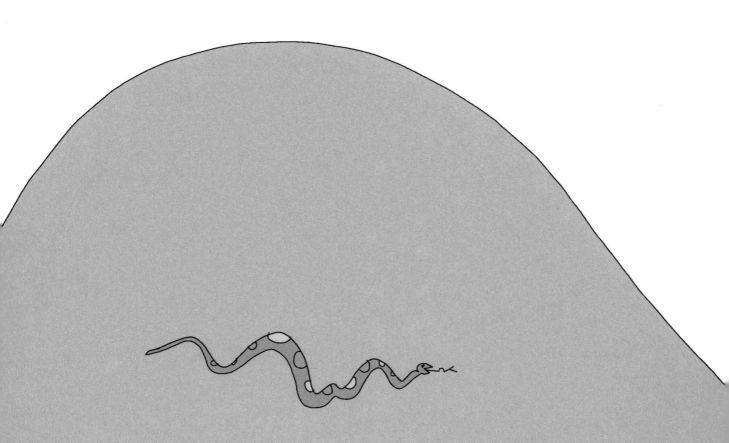

# Hits the Beach

## And Other Wild Adventures

Published by Baker Books
a division of Baker Book House Company
P.O. Box 6287, Grand Rapids, MI 49516-6287

Printed in the United States of America

**Library of Congress Cataloging-in-Publication Data**

Briscoe, Jill.
    Paul hits the beach : and other wild adventures / by Jill and Stuart Briscoe ; pictures & cartoons by Russ Flint.
      p.  cm.
    Summary: Retellings of stories from the New Testament about Peter, Paul, Timothy, James, and John are accompanied by "Let's Pretend" stories, "Neat Facts," plays, and songs.
    ISBN 0-8010-4202-X
1. Paul, the Apostle, Saint—Juvenile literature.  2. Bible stories, English—N.T. Acts.  3. Bible stories, English—N.T. Epistles.  4. Bible stories, English—N.T. Revelation.  5. Drama in Christian education.  6. Bible plays. [1. Bible stories—N.T.] I. Briscoe, D. Stuart.  II. Flint, Russ, ill.  III. Title.
BS2506.5.B65  1997
225.9′2—dc20
                                  96-38563

An accompanying tape (ISBN 0-8010-3017-X) is available from the publisher. It features a children's group singing all the songs in the four books and the Briscoes reading selections from the "Let's Pretend" and "Let's Make a Video" sections.

This book is produced in cooperation with Alive Communications, Inc., 1465 Kelly Johnson Blvd., Suite 320, Colorado Springs, CO 80920.

# CONTENTS

We gratefully appreciate the following people who made this project a delight:

**Betty De Vries,** a wise and skillful editor, whose vision for a children's book coincided with ours and whose skill far exceeded our abilities

**Kappie Griesell,** who so diligently dug out the Neat Facts

**Larry Moore,** who took our words and added his delightful music that sets our feet tapping and our hearts singing

**Russ Flint,** whose art is so entrancing and interesting that we wonder if anyone will read our text

To
**our grandchildren,**
whom we love so dearly

May this book
bring delight to your hearts
and more love
and appreciation
for the God whom we serve.

# There's something special about this book

 To

catch by surprise
and to surprise with joy
freshen
and excite new attention
in the old, old story

 To

peek around the corner of a verse
and delight to see
who is coming

 To

smell the smells
admire the rich clothes
and glimpse the colors
of worlds different from ours

 To

break the bread of life
into small enough pieces
for young minds
to thoroughly digest

 To

tell of Jesus—
from Genesis to Revelation

 To

discover truths old and new
young and old
child and adult
together

 **To**

experience
with laughter and tears
simple retelling of old stories
allowing imagination
to refresh favorite events
using songs and simple dramas
to promote understanding

 **To**

know God better
love God more

 **To**

share these discoveries
with a lost, hurting world
of children
and adults

 **To**

this end
authors
artist
composer
publisher

invite you to enjoy
Book 4, *Paul Hits the Beach: And Other Wild Adventures*!

# *Letter to Parents*

Now that our three children are in their "thirty somethings," we realize we have been parents an aggregate of over a hundred years.

There's more!

As our children have produced nine grandchildren, at last count, we have accumulated almost forty years of grandparenting.

So you could say we have a vested interest in children.

We enjoy telling stories to youngsters, answering their questions, hearing them laugh, and watching their eyes light up with understanding. There's nothing quite like a fire, a cozy chair, a child, an adult, and a good children's book.

"Read us a story, Papa Stu," elicits a special response, especially when I have a good story available.

"Tell us about Daniel and the lions, Grandma," will energize even a fatigued senior citizen.

With these things in mind, we started to work on this project. We wanted to produce something that would convey the old, old story in a new and fresh way. Our intention was that children, long familiar with Bible stories, would be drawn to them once again because they were presented differently. How differently? Well, we are firm believers in children having their own imaginative capabilities and their special brand of humor. So "straight stories" are immediately followed by imaginative, humorous "Let's Pretend" tales.

Parents may be surprised to learn that Jonah's whale was called Wally and that the seagulls observing his watery excursion were called Bea Gull and Dee Gull, and that mountains talk to giraffes, but children will take it in their stride. And they'll love Russ Flint's pictures and cartoons and funny little sketches. They'll laugh and so will you.

Our primary aim is to lead young children and adults alike to a wider knowledge of the Book of Books. May you find these books interesting, endearing, entertaining, educational, and inspiring.

Happy reading,

Jill and Stuart

Book 3, *Jesus Makes a Major Comeback*, tells the story of Luke, the man who wrote the Gospel of Luke and the Book of Acts. Luke wanted his friend Theophilus to believe that Jesus was the Son of God. Luke watched Jesus preach and teach and heal and help people. Luke also watched Jesus suffer and die. One of the most exciting things Luke watched was Jesus' ascension into heaven.

So Luke begins his second book, the Book of Acts, with that story. The last orders Jesus gave his disciples were: "Go into all the world and tell people about me." Jesus wanted the disciples to make sure that everybody in the whole world knew that he had died for their sins and was alive again. The disciples wondered how they could possibly let everybody know. Jesus said that he would send the Holy Spirit, who would be with them and would help them to be brave and do what Jesus wanted them to do. Then Jesus left the disciples. They watched him go up in the air until a cloud covered him and they could no longer see him.

# THE
# ACTS OF THE
# APOS

Luke then tells how the Holy Spirit came on Pentecost and one of the disciples, Peter, preached a powerful sermon about Jesus' life. This was the same Peter who was so afraid that three times he said he never knew Jesus. Many people believed what Peter said was true, but other people were jealous and thought about ways to get rid of Peter.

Not everyone liked the idea of people believing in Jesus. Saul wanted to kill every Christian he found. But God took care of the new Christians. God knew just how to make Saul into a Christian. And he did. Suddenly, Saul, the man who wanted to kill Christians, was working as hard as he could to tell as many people as he could find that Jesus was the Son of God. Saul's name was changed to Paul. Luke and Paul went on several missionary trips together. Luke tells about many, many things that happened on those trips. Paul's final days were spent in Rome. While in prison there, he wrote many letters to his helpers and to churches he had helped to grow.

## PETER

One day after Jesus had gone back to heaven and God the Father had sent the Holy Spirit to help the apostles, Peter and John were going to the temple to pray. Christians living then went to the temple at three o'clock in the afternoon. The temple had many gates. They were called by different names. A crippled man was begging by the one called "Beautiful." The crippled man didn't know it, but a beautiful thing was about to happen to him that very day.

Seeing the man, Peter said, "Look at me." The man looked up happily, hoping for some money. Instead, Peter and John were able to give him something that money couldn't buy.

"I don't have any silver and gold to give you," Peter said, "but in the name of Jesus—walk!"

Then Peter bent down and helped the man to his feet. The man's feet and ankles became strong and he began to walk about—even jump up and down.

Imagine what he must have felt. He had never, ever walked in his whole life—even when he was a small child. The man went leaping and jumping through the Beautiful Gate. He went straight into the temple.

"Isn't this the man who sits begging at the gate?" asked a man. "Isn't he the one who's been crippled from birth?"

"It can't be," replied a woman. "This man just looks like him."

"It is the man!" shouted a boy. "I pass him every day."

"How does he stand, walk, and jump?" gasped a shopkeeper.

By now a crowd of people had run up to the man who was holding on to Peter and John as if he never wanted them to go. Everyone was staring at the two apostles as if they had done a great miracle.

"Why are you staring at us?" Peter asked them. "It is in Jesus' great power—not our own—that we have done this."

Peter knew this was a good time to tell the crowd more about the Lord. "It is in Jesus' name this man has been healed," he explained. "Jesus is the one you wanted crucified even though Pilate wanted to let him go. You killed the author of life, but God raised him from the dead. We have seen him since and that is the truth. If you are sorry for what you did," Peter continued, "he will forgive you."

The leaders of the Jews were angry at what had happened, and they put Peter and John in jail. The next day they threatened them and said they would be punished if they talked about Jesus again. The problem was the man who had been healed was standing in front of the crowd too. Everyone could see him for themselves.

"Why did you put us in jail for being kind to a cripple?" Peter asked them. "Anyway, we must obey God before we obey you!"

Peter and John were brave and bold. The leaders were amazed and let the apostles go. The first thing Peter and John did was to report to their own people everything that had happened. All the believers praised God and prayed for strength and courage to go on serving the Lord.

Then the room began to shake because God's Holy Spirit came to all of them. The believers felt very brave and quite ready for the work that Jesus had for them to do. Peter became a leader of the church. He preached the good news about Jesus to many, many people. He was a brave and faithful follower of Jesus.

You Obey God because you are his children. 1 Peter 1:14 TLB

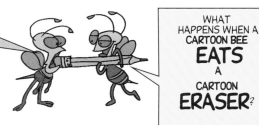

# Let's Pretend

## PIGS & LOBSTERS

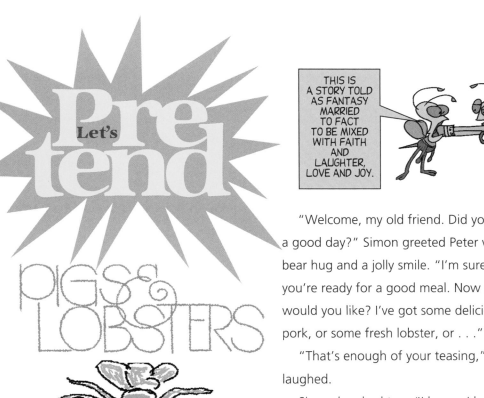

It had been a long hard day. Peter was tired as he climbed the narrow path to his friend Simon's home. "I wish he lived closer to town," Peter grumbled. "But I suppose he has to live away from the other homes because of the smell." Simon was a tanner and had all sorts of animal skins drying on racks around his house. The hot sun made the skins smell, and some days the smell was quite strong.

"Welcome, my old friend. Did you have a good day?" Simon greeted Peter with a bear hug and a jolly smile. "I'm sure you're ready for a good meal. Now what would you like? I've got some delicious pork, or some fresh lobster, or . . ."

"That's enough of your teasing," Peter laughed.

Simon laughed too. "I know, I know, you're a strict old Jew. I know we can't eat any of those things. I was just having a joke with you. But seriously, someday you must explain to me why Moses said certain animals and birds were unclean and we shouldn't eat them."

"One of these days I will," Peter replied. "But if you don't mind, I'd like to rest for a while on the roof top."

"Good idea!" Simon responded. "Up there the sea air is fresh and the orange blossom is sweet." Then with a grin he added, "Can't smell the smelly skins there either."

Peter climbed the stairs to the flat roof, quickly washed in the cool water provided for him, lay down in a hammock, and fell fast asleep. Then he had the strangest dream. He seemed to be looking up into the bright blue sky when a shiny white dot appeared. It grew bigger and bigger until it looked like a great tent had collapsed. As it came so close that he thought he could touch it, Peter saw it was a giant sheet full of pigs and lobsters, and all kinds of other animals. Those were the creatures Moses said were unclean.

"Rise, Peter, kill and eat!" a strong voice said. Peter knew it was the Lord.

"Lord, you know I can't eat pigs and lobsters and such things. They are not suitable for a Jewish stomach. Moses said so. Surely, Lord, you know that!"

"If I say they're fit to eat, don't you say they aren't," the Lord replied quite strongly.

With that the sheet shot back into the sky as if it had been propelled by a rocket. Peter was really worried.

*What's going on?* he wondered. He didn't have long to think about it because the sheet was returning at a great speed. *Now what?* Peter thought. The same thing happened again, and then the whole episode was repeated a third time.

*I guess the Lord is trying to tell me something,* Peter thought as he dreamed. *Is he telling me that I should do things he wants me to do even when I don't want to do them?*

As he dreamed on, he heard another voice, "Peter, Peter." The voice was not the Lord's. Peter felt himself being shaken, and he awoke with a start to see his friend Simon violently shaking the hammock.

"Wake up, old sleepyhead. You were miles away muttering about pork and lobster and something about the Lord telling you to do what you don't want to do! I'm sorry if I spoiled your dreams by teasing you about unclean food."

"I had a strange dream, Simon," Peter started to say.

Simon interrupted, "Well, I've a strange request for you as well! Downstairs are three Romans who say that their leader Cornelius, a famous Roman soldier, wants you to come to his house to tell him about Jesus. Cornelius says that the Lord told him to ask you to come."

"Oh, I could never do that," Peter replied. "Cornelius is not a Jew; he's a Gentile. I couldn't go into an unclean place like a Gentile home."

Simon smiled and asked, "Even if the Lord said it was all right?" It was just as if the Holy Spirit used Simon's words to show Peter that God was talking not just about pigs and lobsters, but people. If God said it

was all right to eat certain food, it was certainly all right to meet certain people.

So Peter did something he never thought he would do. No, he didn't have pork for supper—he went to the home of Cornelius and talked about Jesus, the Son of God. Cornelius and his family listened to every word and became happy, joyful Christians.

God was pleased to welcome these Gentile believers into his family. And Peter? Well, he finally understood the meaning of his strange dream. He was happy, too, and ready now to do whatever God wanted done.

# Peter & Me

When we hear some good news or get something special, we can't wait to tell our friends and anyone we meet about it. We get so excited. We just have to talk about it.

Andrew couldn't wait to tell Peter the good news that Jesus had come. They were two very happy brothers spending time with Jesus. Later Peter spent his life preaching to many, many people, telling them about Jesus. You know the good news about Jesus too. Are you excited about that? Are you telling anyone about Jesus?

On the day of Pentecost, 3,000 people said they believed that Jesus was the Son of God. That's how the first church was formed. If your room at school has desks for 30 students, you would need 100 rooms that size to hold all the new followers of Jesus.

Jesus came to earth quietly as a baby. The Holy Spirit came with a very loud sound like the blowing of a mighty wind, with tongues of fire, and with the power to help all the people to talk in other languages. The first Christians heard the sound, saw the tongues of fire, and spoke about it. Imagine going to church being able to talk in one language, and then in a minute, without spending any time studying, being able to talk and understand many languages.

Peter and the other disciples needed roads on which to travel to other cities to tell people about Jesus. No problem! The Romans who ruled the world when Jesus lived were road builders. They had already built 53,000 miles of road. We can still find small parts of these roads today.

WHAT IS A **DIS-CI-PLE?**

A DISCIPLE IS A STUDENT WHO OBEYS HIS TEACHER.

WHAT IS AN **APOSTLE?**

APOSTLE COMES FROM A GREEK WORD THAT MEANS SOMEONE WHO IS SENT OUT.

Fancy Footnotes

# Let's Make a Video about

*Cast:* Sixteen soldiers, angel, Peter, crowd at Mary's house (man, woman, boy), Mary, Rhoda, Herod, centurion

*Scenes:* Prison and Mary's house.

| | |
|---|---|
| *Narrator* | The church was in trouble. King Herod was killing its leaders. He saw this pleased the Jews who hated the Christians, so he had Peter arrested and put in prison. |

*Enter sixteen soldiers who surround Peter and take up positions.*

| | |
|---|---|
| *Peter* | Why do you have to guard me with sixteen soldiers? I am not a murderer or some sort of dangerous criminal. I am a humble follower of Jesus of Nazareth. |
| *Centurion* | You are a leader of the Christians—troublemakers, all of them. Once the feast of the Passover is over, Herod intends to bring you to public trial. |
| *Soldier* | And you know what happened at the time of the Passover feast. Your precious Jesus was put on trial and crucified, so it doesn't look very good for you! |
| *Peter* | Well, you need not be afraid that I will be violent or cause you a problem. If it is God's will that I die for my faith, that's how it will be. But if God wants to set me free, he will rescue me no matter how many soldiers are guarding me. |

*Peter goes to sleep, lights down.*

| | |
|---|---|
| *Narrator* | Meanwhile, in the city at John Mark's house, John's mother, Mary, gets the house ready for a prayer meeting. |

*Lights up, people arrive, greet each other, settle in to pray.*

| | |
|---|---|
| *Mary* | Welcome, all of you, in the name of the Lord Jesus. I am glad you have come to pray for our leader. They tell us Peter is in the strongest prison guarded by four squads of four soldiers. Herod intends to bring him to public trial after the Passover feast is over. |
| *Man* | We must pray: O Lord God, you who brought Daniel out of the lions' den, see fit to rescue Peter from the lions' den too! |

*Lights down, freeze.*
*Lights up on prison. Peter is asleep between two soldiers. He is chained.*

| | |
|---|---|
| *Narrator* | Now the Passover feast is over and Herod decides to put Peter on trial. Suddenly an angel of the Lord appears. (Enter angel.) A light shines in the cell. The angel tries to awaken Peter, but he is so soundly asleep he is snoring and can't wake up properly. The angel hits him quite hard on the back and wakes him up. |
| *Peter* | (startled) What . . . who . . . who are you? (Peter's chains fall off; the soldiers stay asleep.) |
| *Angel* | Quick! Get up! Put on your clothes and sandals, wrap your cloak around you, and follow me. |

*Peter does so and follows the angel a little way. Two squads of soldiers stand in guarding position at the gates of the prison. The angel leads Peter through both sets, opens the gates* (mime) *and walks a little farther. Peter follows as if in a dream. The angel leaves him, and Peter wakes up.*

| | |
|---|---|
| *Peter* | (startled) Now I know this is real. I'm not dreaming! The Lord has sent his angel and rescued me from Herod's clutches and from all my enemies. But where shall I go? I know where people will be—at the prayer meeting in Mary's house. |

*Arrives at house; lights up on prayer meeting; Peter knocks and Rhoda comes to door.*

| | |
|---|---|
| *Rhoda* | Who is it? |
| *Peter* | It's me, Peter! |
| *Rhoda* | It can't be. You're in prison! |
| *Peter* | Open the door, Rhoda. It's really me. |
| *Rhoda* | It can't be you. We've just been praying for you. |
| *Peter* | It *is* me! God sent his angel and rescued me. Open the door! |

*Rhoda believes, but is so excited she spins around, does a little dance, but doesn't open the door.*

Peter          Let me in!

Rhoda          It's Peter, it's Peter!

Mary           Peter who?

Rhoda          Peter, Peter. You know, our beloved leader, the one we've been praying for.

*Loud knocking.*

Woman          You're out of your mind.

Rhoda          I'm not. I tell you—it is him. Listen!

*More knocking.*

Man            It must be his angel!

Boy            Angels don't knock on doors. They go right through them!

*More loud knocks; Peter is getting desperate to get inside.*

Peter          Hurry! Let me in! Let me in!

Boy            Sirs, we have been praying for his release. Maybe God is answering our prayers right now.

*Two or three persons run to the door and open it. There is Peter. Everyone gathers around and excitedly greets him, asking him to tell what happened.*

Peter          Quiet, then, and I'll tell you my story.

*He does so quickly, excitedly, giving God credit. As scene fades Peter says good-bye.*

Peter          Tell James and the brothers all about this.

*All exit.*
*Lights up on prison scene. Soldiers wake up and find the prisoner gone. The soldiers are frightened, petrified.*

Herod          *(enters, furious)* We have searched for the prisoner. You have let him get away from me, and by now he is in hiding. *(screams)* I will have you all punished. Take them away!

*The guards are led off by other guards.*

Narrator       God rescued Peter from Herod's hands. God heard the prayers of his people as he always does when his children are in trouble. He doesn't always rescue them as he rescued Peter, but he promises to be with them whatever happens and, one day, to take them to be with him in heaven. When we all get to heaven, we will be safe forever, because heaven is a place Herod and other wicked people can never go.

THESE TWO PAGES ARE SCARY!

YEAH! NO PICTURES!

29

## PAUL'S LIFE

When Jesus died on the cross, he finished the work of salvation his Father had given him to do and was ready to go back to heaven. Jesus asked the disciples to work for him on earth. He promised to send a helper who would always be with them. The disciples loved Jesus and wanted to tell everybody about him. But the work was hard to do without Jesus. They really needed the helper Jesus had promised them.

Ten days after Jesus went back to heaven, he sent the Holy Spirit to help the disciples. More and more people listened to the disciples when they told about Jesus. Many people joined the disciples and became believing Christians.

At first the believers met in homes because they didn't have church buildings. Sometimes the believers met in the beautiful big temple. So many people began to believe in Jesus that the leaders who had him killed got very upset. "Why," they said, "it's worse now than when he was alive!" Of course, Jesus *was* alive in his people, and that is why so many wonderful things were happening.

One of the main leaders of the Jews was named Saul. He had been taught by a wise and wonderful teacher, Gamaliel. Saul knew the Scriptures inside and out. He didn't believe Jesus was the promised one all the Jews were waiting for. Saul was a man of action, so he decided he would put a stop to all this teaching and preaching about Jesus. He wanted to arrest, imprison, and maybe kill anyone who believed that Jesus was the Son of God. He got permission from the Jewish leaders to do this, and soon Saul

was traveling all over the country arresting as many of Jesus' disciples as he could. Everyone was afraid of Saul.

Stephen, a believer, was arrested by the Jewish leaders and told to stop preaching about Jesus. Of course, Stephen wouldn't stop, so the leaders said Stephen had to be stoned to death. Saul watched this and even held the coats of the people who were stoning Stephen. Saul wondered how Stephen could pray for the people who were throwing stones at him. Jesus, the risen Lord, was helping Stephen, but Saul didn't know that.

Saul wanted to go to Damascus, a city where many Christians lived. As he and his friends were walking toward that city, a bright light suddenly lit up everything around them, even though the sun was high in the sky. Saul was blinded by the great light. He fell to the ground. The people walking with him were very, very afraid.

Suddenly a voice spoke to Saul, "Saul, Saul, why do you persecute me?"

Saul asked the voice, "Who are you, Lord?" The mysterious voice from heaven answered, "I am Jesus."

Jesus had met Saul right there on the road to Damascus, and Saul

changed his mind about who Jesus was.

From that time on, Saul (soon he used the Greek form of his name, *Paul*) stopped persecuting Christians. God had new, exciting, but dangerous work for Paul to do. With God's help Paul became the first great missionary who told many people the good news about Jesus—that he was truly the Son of God, the Promised One, the Messiah.

The Acts of the Lord spread through the whole region. word 13:49

# Let's Pretend

## PONTIUS PUBLIUS PLUTO, the PHILIPPIAN PRISON GUARD

THIS IS A STORY TOLD AS FANTASY MARRIED TO FACT TO BE MIXED WITH FAITH AND LAUGHTER LOVE AND JOY.

PHOO PHOO PHOO PHOO PHOO PHOO PHOO PHOO PHOO PHOO PHOO PHOO PHOO PHOO PHOO PHOO PHOO PHOO PHOO PHOO PHOO PHOO PHOO PHOO PHOO PHOO PHOO PHOOOOO

Pontius Publius Pluto couldn't sleep.

He was very tired, but he still couldn't sleep.

He'd had a busy day looking after the Philippi prison. Two men from out of town had been brought to him.

Some of the important people in town had said to him, "Put them in the prison, Pontius Publius Pluto. They have been causing trouble in the marketplace. They are teaching things that are not true, and we don't like it. Lock them up!"

Pontius Publius Pluto had seen a lot of troublemakers in the many years he had been a soldier and a prison guard. But these men didn't look like troublemakers.

"Beat them with rods till their backs bleed!" the important people had shouted.

So while the crowds watched, the soldiers tore off the men's clothes and beat them.

Pontius Publius Pluto had heard two of the men talk. They were telling people that someone called Jesus had been crucified and then had risen from the dead. They said he was the Son of God. Pontius Publius Pluto didn't believe any of this, and he wondered why everybody was getting so upset about it. He was thinking hard about all these things.

But that wasn't why he couldn't sleep.

"Put them in the worst cell. Fasten their feet in the heavy wooden stocks. Tie their hands to the wall with chains. Don't let them escape or we'll punish you, Pontius Publius Pluto," the important people had said to him.

Pontius Publius Pluto didn't think it was very fair that the men had been beaten and put in prison, but he didn't let that worry him very much. It wasn't any of his

33

business. If he could stay out of trouble, he didn't care about other people's troubles. But that wasn't why he couldn't sleep.

The men's backs were very sore. The chains hurt their wrists and the stocks hurt their feet. But that didn't bother Pontius Publius Pluto, the big, cruel man who had hurt many people when they were in his prison. That wasn't why he couldn't sleep.

It was the singing. The two men were singing at the top of their voices.

That was why he couldn't sleep!

"Be quiet!" he shouted at the top of his voice. "Be quiet or I'll come down there and beat you some more." The jailor put a pillow over his head and soon he was snoring.

Still the singing went on.

"Praise the name of Jesus," they sang. "O, dear Jesus, bless these poor men who lie in these prison cells. Bless the important people of this town who don't love you. And bless Pontius Publius Pluto." On and on they sang and prayed. And they were singing at the top of their voices. The noise got louder and louder.

"They're praying for my husband!" said Mrs. Pluto, who had awakened because of all the noise.

"For my husband? They're praying for him? I don't believe it," she said and wished they would be quiet so that she could get some sleep. Her husband was still snoring.

The next minute there was a loud rumbling. The bed began to shake. The lamp fell on the floor. The walls began to crumble. Pontius Publius Pluto fell out of bed. Mrs. Pluto fell out of bed on top of him.

"It's an earthquake!" he shouted. His mouth was full of dust. The ceiling collapsed and the floor was swaying.

"My prisoners will escape!" he shouted to his wife.

He grabbed the short sword he always kept by his bed. *If the prisoners have escaped, the important people will kill me,* he thought. *I'm so frightened, I think I'll kill myself now.*

Then he heard a shout from the one of the cells.

"Pontius Publius Pluto, don't worry about a thing. Everything is going to be all right. We're all here. No one has escaped. Our chains are loose but we didn't want to get you into trouble. So we didn't run away."

Paul, one of the two men who had been singing, was talking to Pontius Publius Pluto, who had never met men like this before. They sang in their cell. They prayed for their enemies. They didn't escape when they could have. They didn't swear when their backs were beaten. They were wonderful men.

*I know what makes them so different! It must be this Jesus. The Spirit of Jesus lives in them,* thought Pontius Publius Pluto, as he climbed over piles of stones and stocks and chains and dust to what used to be the cell that held Paul and Silas.

"Tell me, you two men," he asked, "what must I do to become like you? I am not a good man. I am not a kind man. Can your Jesus send his Spirit into my life?"

"He certainly can," replied Paul cheerfully. "You must talk to him about your sins and tell him you are sorry. You must thank him for dying for you and ask him to send his Spirit into your life."

"How do I do that?" asked Pontius Publius Pluto.

"Pray with me," Paul said. And there in the dust and rubble and piles of stones and stocks, Pontius Publius Pluto, the cruel prison guard of Philippi, became a Christian.

"Now what do I do?" he asked after they had prayed.

"Well, you could get some water and help us clean up our bleeding backs, if you don't mind," Silas suggested.

"Certainly!" said Pontius Publius Pluto. "But would you tell all my family what you've just told me?"

"We'd love to," said Paul. "Would you like to wash our wounds while we tell them?"

So that's what they did, and all the family of Pontius Publius Pluto became Christians that night. When the important people of the city came to see if the prisoners were safe, they couldn't believe their eyes—or their ears. The family of Pontius Publius Pluto were singing, "Praise the name of Jesus."

# Paul & Me

Paul had to change his mind when he became a Christian. This must have been hard for him to do because he was the sort of person who had made up his mind about so many things. But God wanted Paul to change his mind about some of the wrong things he was doing. So he did.

Do you have trouble changing your mind? God wants us to be willing to do that if we behave badly or in a way he doesn't like. If God shows us something needs changing, we need to change it. He will help us, just as he helped Paul.

# tuff Neat stuff Neat

Before Paul became a worker for Jesus, he was a very strict Pharisee. The Pharisees spent a lot of time trying to obey all the rules that were in the first five books of the Bible and the thousands of rules people had added to God's rules. Some of the rules the Pharisees had seem silly. Here are a few of them:

A person could walk only 3,000 meters (9,000 feet or a little more than a mile and a half) on the Sabbath day. But if a person was making a dish that called for many ingredients, one ingredient could be picked up at a nearby house, another ingredient picked up at a house about a mile and a half away (or closer than that), and so on, until all the ingredients were picked up. The person could return home, mix all the stuff together, and then the dish could be delivered to another house, even if that house was almost a mile and a half away. So if one wanted to take a long walk on a Sunday, much longer than the mile and a half allowed by the rules, he could pick up an egg at one house, some salt at a second house, some pepper at a third house, some cheese at a fourth house, some onion or garlic at a fifth house, and so on, even if the houses were almost a mile and a half away, until he had all the stuff for one stupendous omelet. Then he could go back home, make the omelet and deliver it to another friend's house that could be as much as a mile and a half away.

If a house was burning on the Sabbath day, a man could not put out the fire, but he could go in, put on all the good clothes he could wear, and wrap himself with whatever he could. Another ruling said he could carry out only eighteen things but could go back for more.

weaving, making two loops, weaving two threads, separating two threads, tying a knot, loosening a knot, sewing two stitches, or tearing to sew two stitches.

On the Sabbath day no one could climb a tree, ride a beast, swim in water, clap hands, slap thighs, or stamp with feet.

These kinds of work could not be done on the Sabbath: sowing, plowing, reaping, binding sheaves, threshing, winnowing, cleaning crops, grinding, sifting, kneading, baking, shearing wool, washing or beating or dyeing wool, spinning,

The Pharisees were also concerned about things that were "clean" or "unclean," and most of the time they were not talking about dirty things but items they considered not proper to use or eat:

Flat, round plates or dishes were clean. If they were rectangular, they could be unclean.

Any article (jug or pot or jar) that might be used to hold something or carry something might be called unclean.

A ring worn by men could be unclean; a ring for cattle or utensils was not.

A curved horn might be unclean; a straight horn was not. But if the mouthpiece of a horn was made of metal, the horn could be unclean even if it was a straight horn.

If a person with unwashed hands ate a fig cake and then put his fin-

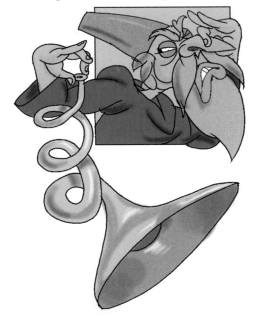

gers into his mouth to take out the small stones, the fig cake became unclean. Another ruling said that if a person turned the fig cake over in his mouth it became unclean.

There were general rules as well:

A man could not say, "How much is this thing?" if he did not wish to buy it.

An unmarried man could not be a teacher of children, nor could a woman be a teacher of children.

A person with any kind of a blemish or spot or physical or mental disability could not serve as a priest.

Meat could not be boiled in milk.

A Nazarite could not cut his hair. He could rub it or scratch it, but he could not comb it. Neither could he rub it with earth since that made the hair fall out.

Widows could be married on Thursday. Other weddings could be held on Wednesday.

Scrolls had to be read reverently. A man did not fulfill his obligation if he read the scroll in the wrong order, read it by heart, or read it in Aramaic or any other language.

# Let's Make a Video about

Your Family Video Theater

## Uncle Paul's Life Is Saved

*Paul*

Cast: *Tabitha, Amos, a man, a Pharisee, a Jew, mother of Amos, guard, Paul, centurion, commander, soldier*
Scenes: *Dining area, home of Amos and mother, jail cell, commander's room.*

| | |
|---|---|
| Tabitha | Amos, Amos, take the bread to the table. |
| Amos | Yes, Tabitha. *(Takes food to room where a crowd of men are making plans to kill Paul.)* |
| Man | We come here to eat together and plan to get rid of this fellow, Paul. . . . |

*Amos drops plate of bread in shock.*

| | |
|---|---|
| Pharisee | What's wrong, boy? You can take that bread back to the kitchen. We won't be needing it. |
| Jew | We are with you, brother. There are forty of us who will swear not to eat or drink until we have killed this troublemaker who spreads his Jesus stories everywhere. |

*Amos picks up bread and plate and runs back to his friend.*

| | |
|---|---|
| Amos | Tabitha, they don't want any bread tonight. Can . . . can I leave now? I have something I must do. |
| Tabitha | These men! First they want to eat, then they don't. All right, run along then, Amos. |

*Amos exits, runs home to Mother.*

| | |
|---|---|
| Amos | Mother, Uncle Paul is in great danger! The Jews are planning to kill him! |
| Mother | Amos, go to Uncle Paul. He's being held in the Roman barracks. They will let you in to give him some food. |
| Amos | But, Mother—I'm scared! You know I've always been scared of soldiers and fighting and things like that. |

| | |
|---|---|
| *Mother* | Amos, you'll just have to go and do it scared then! Sometimes that's what we have to do. |
| *Amos* | Well, that doesn't seem fair, Mother. Maybe if we pray, God will stop me from being so frightened, and then I'll do it. |
| *Mother* | We can certainly pray, Amos, but what happens if the feelings don't go away? If we only do what we "feel" good about, so many things will not be done. Often it's hard and even dangerous to do what's right, but we need to go ahead anyway. |
| *Amos* | Oh! Mother! I'll . . . I'll go. |
| *Mother* | I feel awful sending you, Amos. Maybe I could go. |
| *Amos* | The soldiers would never let you in. They won't stop a small boy though. |
| *Mother* | Then go, and God be with you. |

*Amos takes food from his mother and goes to Paul. Match action to narrative as Amos creeps along the street.*

| | |
|---|---|
| *Amos* | Oooh! It's scary. The shadows look like soldiers waiting to pounce on me. |

*Crash! Amos nearly jumps out of his skin. He freezes and then goes on.*

| | |
|---|---|
| *Amos* | Oooh! I hate this. My heart is beating so loudly the soldiers are bound to hear it. |

*He arrives at the gate and timidly speaks to the guard.*

| | |
|---|---|
| *Amos* | Please, sir, I have brought some food from my mother for my Uncle Paul. He's your prisoner. |

*Guard looks in basket, nods to let him in, and takes him to Paul who is sitting in his cell.*

| | |
|---|---|
| *Paul* | *(greets his nephew)* Why, Amos, how did you . . . |
| *Amos* | Uncle Paul, there's no time to waste. The Jews are planning to kill you. I heard it with my own ears. They didn't know I was your nephew, and so they talked freely in front of me. |
| *Paul* | They can do nothing to harm me unless God allows it. But wait—*(calls centurion)* Centurion! Take this young man to your commander. Amos has something to tell him. Good-bye, Amos, and thank you. |
| *Amos* | *(hugs Paul)* I'll pray for you, Uncle Paul. *(to centurion)* I wish my heart would stop jumping around. I've never talked to a Roman commander before. |

| | |
|---|---|
| *Centurion* | Don't be afraid, young man. We want to protect Paul. Even though he's a Jew, he's also a Roman citizen. |

*Amos meets the commander.*

| | |
|---|---|
| *Centurion* | Commander, Sir, this young man has something to tell you. Paul the prisoner asked me to bring him to you. |
| *Commander* | Well, what is it? |
| *Amos* | *(scared)* Please, Sir, I overheard a plan to kill my uncle. The Jews are going to ask you to bring him to their leaders tomorrow. They'll have some excuse about needing to meet with him. Please, Sir, don't do it, because more than forty of them have planned an ambush. I heard them say they won't have breakfast, lunch, or supper, or even snacks until they've killed Uncle Paul. |
| *Commander* | *(kindly)* Thank you for telling me, young man. You can go now, but don't tell anyone you've reported this to me. I'll protect Paul. |
| *Amos* | Oh, thank you, thank you, Sir. |

*Amos exits.*

| | |
|---|---|
| *Commander* | *(to centurion)* Get a detachment of 200 soldiers, 70 horsemen, and 200 spearmen ready. We're going to fool those Jews. Tonight we will move Paul to a place where he will be safe. Governor Felix wants to talk with Paul and we'll see to it that the governor gets his wish. Go, quickly now. I can just see the look on the faces of those Jews tomorrow. We've out-smarted them again. |
| *Soldier* | Excuse me for asking you, Sir, but why spend so much money and make such a fuss over a rabble rousing Jew? Maybe he deserves to be given up to his own people. |
| *Commander* | I've a hunch the man is innocent. Anyway, he's got Roman citizenship. |
| *Soldier* | Oh, Sir, I didn't know. I'll see to it, Sir. |
| *Amos* | *(back home, to mother)* So that's what happened, Mother. The commander was àlready planning how he was going to save Uncle Paul from those forty Jews. He really is in the Lord's hands. I could feel that Jesus was with me when I talked to the commander. |
| *Mother* | Well done, Amos. I prayed and Jesus helped you. Uncle Paul's life was spared. God has everything under control. |

There are twenty-seven books in the New Testament; twenty-one are letters, or as they are sometimes called, epistles. Thirteen of these letters were written by the apostle Paul. We know this because long ago the writer of a letter would put his or her name right at the beginning, followed by the names of the people to whom the letter was addressed. So when Paul wrote to the Romans, he started his letter with the words, "Paul, a servant of Jesus Christ . . . to all in Rome." Paul's name is at the beginning of thirteen letters in the New Testament.

Sometimes Paul wrote a letter to the people of the church in a city such as Rome or Corinth. He wrote other letters to just one person, such as Timothy or Titus. Usually when Paul wrote to a church in a city it was because he had preached the gospel there and helped to start the church. This meant that he loved the people of that church and was interested in how they were doing since they had become Christians. Paul knew that new Christians are like babies who need someone to look after them, so Paul tried to do this even though he wasn't with them. Paul also wrote to other people to show them how to help the people in the churches while he was away.

Sometimes some bad men came to the churches after Paul had been there and told the people things that were not right. When Paul heard about it, he was very upset. If Paul could not travel right away to the city where they were having a problem, he would write a letter to the church telling them not to believe the wrong things these people said. Paul knew that he had told the people the truth. And sometimes he would hear that the people who were new Christians were doing some things that were not right and he wrote to tell them what they should do instead.

Paul liked to have young men such as Timothy and Titus work with him so he could send them to differ-

PAUL'S L

ent places to look after the new churches. These young men sometimes needed help from Paul, so Paul wrote to tell them how to do their work. And one time Paul wrote a short but special letter to his friend Philemon. Paul had met a runaway slave named Onesimus who belonged to Philemon. Onesimus had become a Christian, and Paul said that he should go back to his master. But Onesimus was afraid to go, so Paul wrote a letter asking Philemon to be kind and to look after Onesimus.

When Paul wrote the letters, he did not know that many hundreds of years later we would read them. The people who received the letters did not know that we would see them either. The Holy Spirit helped Paul write the letters; therefore they are helpful to us because they tell us what we need to know about the Lord Jesus and how we should live our lives.

LETTERS

# PAUL'S JOURNEYS

One day Luke and his good friend Paul joined some other men who were traveling to cities across "The Great Sea," today called the Mediterranean Sea. Luke was a doctor who also liked to write, and Paul was going to be a lawyer or a ruler before Jesus changed Paul's mind and asked him to be a missionary. Both Luke and Paul loved Jesus and wanted to tell others about him. Now they were on a big ship and were headed for the city of Rome. At first the sea was calm and the sun was shining. The next day they sailed into a bad storm. The wind blew so strongly that people held on to the railings so they would not be blown over the side of the ship into the water. The waves were higher than a house. The ship would climb to the top of a wave and crash to the bottom of the next one. Then it rolled violently from side to side.

Many times it felt as if the ship was going to tip over. Because the ship was rolling and crashing in the waves, most of the people became ill with seasickness. All the time the wind was howling and shrieking and making a terrible noise. It was scary! It didn't look like the ship was going to make it to dry land. Even the sailors were afraid.

The terrible storm lasted for fourteen days—two weeks. The clouds were so low that the people on the ship could not see the sun by day or the moon by night. The sailors had no idea where they were because the stars by which they found their direction were hidden. They were so terrified that they did not even eat for two weeks.

But Luke's friend Paul was brave because he believed that the Lord would look after them. Luke believed this too. One day Paul shouted above

49

the noise of the wind to the 276 people on the ship. Paul told them that God would look after everybody and they all would be saved. Then Paul told them that they should trust God as he and Luke were doing.

Soon after this the sailors saw some seabirds, so they knew they were getting close to land. Now they were afraid that the ship would crash into some rocks and be smashed into pieces. So all the people prayed as Paul and Luke had told them to. The sailors put out four anchors to stop the boat from being driven onto the rocks by the wind.

The next morning they could see the land. The sailors cut off the anchors, and the wind drove them toward the shore. The sailors managed to steer away from the rocks, and the ship hit a sandbar that stopped it long enough for everybody to get off before the waves pounded the boat to pieces. All the passengers and sailors escaped to the land as God had promised.

But their adventures were not over yet. As Paul was gathering sticks to make a fire so that they could dry their wet clothes, a snake bit him. Everybody thought that Paul would die because the snake was very poisonous. Luke was a doctor but he couldn't help Paul because all the medicines were lost in the shipwreck. God did not let Paul die. In fact, Paul and Luke became very busy caring for many people on the island who were sick. The people were grateful. When the weather improved, it was possible for Luke and Paul and all the other people to continue their trip. They were not afraid to get on another ship because they trusted God to look after them.

When Paul got to Rome, he was allowed to live in a house with a guard for two years until his trial. Paul preached to many people who came to his house, and he spent a lot of time talking to the Roman soldiers who guarded him. They had to listen to him because they couldn't leave their guard post. What did Paul talk about? Jesus, of course. Paul also wrote letters to six more of the new churches he had started in different towns. Those letters are a big part of our New Testament. If we didn't have his wonderful letters in our Bible, we would not know as much about Jesus and the Christian life.

Paul was the greatest missionary who ever lived.

everything with the help of Christ who gives me the strength I need. Philippians 4:13 TLB God asks me to do

50

# Let's Pretend

## THE SNAKE

"I hate snakes! Yuk, get it out of here!" shouted Prisca at her brother Ben.

"SSssssssssss! Sss," Ben teased, dangling a long slimy snake under Prisca's nose. He'd caught the reptile and draped it over a stick before taking it into the big governor's mansion where they lived on the island of Malta.

His sister had climbed on a chair and clutched the heavy curtains that shut out the strong sunlight. She was trying to balance herself. "Get away from me—get!" She pulled so hard at the curtains that they came crashing down and she tumbled off the chair. Curtains, chair, and Prisca were in one tangled heap.

Ben look alarmed. "You all right, Prisca?"

"No, I'm not all right." Suddenly she screamed. "The snake, where's the snake? It's not on your stick, Ben, and it's a poisonous snake. It has those special markings."

Ben didn't know this and now he looked very alarmed. This wasn't turning out the way he had thought it would. He had just wanted to have a little fun at his sister's expense. He thought he would tease her with a small snake that would probably be too scared to come off the stick. Now he would get into trouble because of the curtains and the snake.

"Where did it go?" wailed Prisca. "You know, Ben, it wasn't very clever of you to play with it.

"There it is," screamed Prisca, "by the table leg."

Ben grabbed his mother's favorite jar and dived under the table. He was going to put it over the snake.

"I got it! I got it!" he announced triumphantly. "Stop screaming, Prisca, you'll have the whole Roman fort in here to see what's wrong."

"It's strange no one came with all this commotion," Prisca remarked. She had calmed down and was smoothing her clothes. Now that the snake was trapped, she felt better.

51

"Ben, what will you do with the snake? It really is deadly. We should destroy it."

"Fire is the only way, Prisca, and I know just where there's a nice big bonfire."

Prisca was astonished. "Where? The soldiers hardly ever make a bonfire, just charcoal fires in the courtyard to keep their hands warm."

"I saw soldiers carting piles of wood off in the direction of the beach," Ben replied. "Something's going on down there. I was headed in that direction when I saw the snake and I decided to come and tease you instead."

"That must be where everyone is," said Prisca. "There's no one in the house. I can't imagine what they're all doing by the beach. The weather is awful."

"Let's go and see," suggested Ben. "I can take the snake in the jar. It's got a tight cover on it so the snake can't get out. When the soldiers make the fire big enough I can throw the horrid thing into the fire."

So the children set off for the beach. As soon as they got to a turn in the path, they could see the flames from a huge bonfire leaping high into the sky. There was such a commotion going on. Even though the wind was whipping through the trees and the waves were pounding on the shore, they could hear shouts coming from the place where the bonfire had been lit.

As they came to the point where the path met the beach, Prisca and Ben stopped dead. Ben clutched the jar with the viper imprisoned inside. They looked around in amazement. There were soldiers everywhere, and among them prisoners,

52

wet and bedraggled. Some were lying
down exhausted, still hanging on to
pieces of a wrecked ship they had appar-
ently used to get to land.

Ben ran to his father, Publius, the governor of the island. His father seemed to
be organizing everything.

"What's happened, Father?"

"Shipwreck," responded his father
crisply. "Don't get in the way now, Ben.
We need to dry out these poor men—soldiers and prisoners too. They need food."

"Some are real prisoners," gasped Ben.
"What have they done?"

"All prisoners are somebody's son or
father or husband, whatever they have
done," Publius replied. "Poor wretches,
they are headed for Rome's worst jails. A
little last kindness is the least we can do."

Suddenly, Ben's father caught sight of
the jar Ben was carrying. "What's that?"
he asked. "Why did you bring it out here?
Your mother will be after you if it gets
broken."

"I've got a snake in it. It's poisonous,
though I didn't know it was till Prisca told
me," Ben replied meekly.

"Shake it out of the jar and into the
fire, my son," Publius said. "Do it now!"

A man was gathering brushwood for
the bonfire. He smiled at Prisca and threw
the wood on top of the fire. The flames
flew high into the sky. Ben looked at the
man and realized he was one of the prisoners. The man smiled at the boy.

There was something about the man's
eyes that made Ben want to find out
more about him. He didn't seem to be a
bad man.

Ben stepped up to the roaring flames, quickly pulled the cover off the jar, turned it upside down, and shook it as hard as he could.

Everyone who had been in the water from the shipwreck gathered close to the fire, trying to get warm and dry. Suddenly the snake slithered out of the red hot coals, trying to escape the heat. With a hiss it shot in the direction of the man who had smiled at Ben. The man was putting more wood on the fire.

Prisca screamed, "The snake—look out!"

Ben watched, horrified, as the snake lashed out for the man's hand.

A soldier drew his sword and walked toward the snake. Before he could reach the snake or the man, the forked tongue of the creature had darted out and in and the snake's jaws had closed around the prisoner's hand. Now everyone had seen it, and most of the men recognized it as a deadly snake. There it was, hanging from the man's hand. He stood up and quite calmly shook the snake off into the fire where this time the flames did their work. All eyes were fastened on the prisoner.

"Oh, how horrible!" gasped Prisca, clutching on to her brother. "Now he'll swell up and his eyes will bulge out and he'll choke to death. I saw it happen to one of our servants."

"He must be a murderer," said one of the islanders to a friend. "Though he escaped from the sea, justice has caught up with him now."

By now the prisoner had taken his seat again. He looked quite unconcerned and started to talk with one of the island sol-

diers. He smiled as he talked about a person named Jesus. Prisca and Ben listened and were fascinated.

"It won't take long for the poison to work," whispered Prisca. "He doesn't know what a deadly snake it is. Ben, let's go. That's a horrible way to die and I don't want to watch it."

"No, let's wait," whispered Ben. There was something about the whole thing that made Ben want to stay and help out. Maybe he could get some water to help the poor man as he died.

But Paul (for that was who the prisoner was) didn't die. He didn't even swell up. The islanders, the soldiers, and his fellow prisoners watched closely. They were sure he would suddenly drop dead.

Publius had seen it all too. "He must be a god," whispered his commander. Publius smiled, for while he believed in many gods and thought they might visit humans on earth some day, he didn't think they would visit in the form of a prisoner.

"I'd like to take the man and his companions home with me," said Publius. He had realized Paul had friends with him.

The soldier in charge was happy to let them go for a few days. He was thankful to Paul because Paul had taken charge of the shipwreck and had saved their lives.

Prisca and Ben raced back to the mansion to tell their mother the exciting story.

During the next three months, some wonderful things happened to Ben and Prisca and their family. Paul had laid his hands on Ben and Prisca's grandfather who was deathly ill. Immediately their grandfather was healed. Everyone on the island heard about that and brought other sick people to Paul. The same thing happened to them. No one wanted Paul to leave the island.

All of these things happened because of Jesus, Paul explained. He told them about the carpenter of Nazareth who was the Savior of the world. It was for Jesus' sake Paul himself was a prisoner. Paul explained that he didn't mind that, because it gave him a chance to go to Rome and tell Caesar about Jesus too! The children thought Paul and his friends were the bravest, most wonderful men they had ever met.

Ben and Prisca had tears in their eyes when they eventually had to say good-bye to Paul. But they had found Paul's Jesus for themselves and knew that one day they would meet Paul in heaven around the throne of Jesus.

# Paul & Me

Paul had something wrong with him. We don't know what it was but we do know that three times he asked God to heal him. He called whatever it was his "thorn in the flesh." Instead of healing Paul, God promised Paul strength to cope with the problem. This way Paul would shout to God for help instead of relying on himself.

Sometimes when we have a "thorn in the flesh," something that gives us a lot of pain, or makes us unhappy, or maybe is a handicap, we ask God to take it away, don't we? It's perfectly all right to ask the Lord to do this, but we must be ready to hear him say as he said to Paul, "I won't heal you this time, but I will help you bear it." When we lean on God as we struggle with pain or unhappiness, he becomes very real to us. We can get to know him well. We can even begin to be glad he didn't answer our prayer the way we wanted it answered.

Rome * Thessalonica * Philippi *

Athens * Corinth *

Ephesus *

Antioch *

Cyprus *

Sidon *
Tyre *
Caesarea *

Jerusalem *

lta *

# Paul's Journeys

Do you like to go on long trips? Do you take some of your favorite things with you? Do you like to go to see places where people talk another language? Paul went on three very long and dangerous trips. We call them his missionary journeys. What do you think Paul took with him? Most of the time he had to walk. Sometimes he took a boat.

Paul visited many cities. The Book of Acts lists the names of forty-four cities and islands Paul visited. He visited many cities and islands more than once. Most of these cities are in ruins today or have changed their names. But we can still visit some of these places today. Can you find them on a map?

| | |
|---|---|
| Athens | Malta |
| Caesarea | Rome |
| Cyprus | Sidon |
| Ephesus | Thessalonica |
| Jerusalem | Tyre |

57

Did you know that Paul knew how to make tents? Sometimes he made tents and sold them to make money to buy food or clothes.

Have you ever heard about Mars Hill? Mars was the Roman name for a Greek god. Maybe you know about the planet Mars, which was also named for that god. Or maybe you like to eat a Mars candy bar. Paul used Mars Hill, a rocky hill, as a pulpit or place to preach to the rulers of Athens. Maybe someday you can go to Athens and climb Mars Hill.

# Let's Make a **Video** about

PARTISHIPANTS ARE ENCOURASHED TO EXSHPAND AND IMPROVISH, USHING THISH MASHERIAL ASH A GUIDE. ALLOW SHOR IMASHINATION TO "PEESH AROUND THE CORNER OF THE VERSH" AND SHE WHO ISH COMING.

Your Family Video Theater

**Eutychus**

*Paul*

*Cast:* Eutychus, Mother, Father, Benjamin, woman 1, woman 2, Paul, man

*Scene:* Home of Eutychus and home church where Paul is preaching.

| | |
|---|---|
| *Narrator* | It's sundown on a Sabbath evening in the city of Troas and time for the family to go to church. |
| *Eutychus* | Mother, I learned to count in school today. |
| *Mother* | Good, Eutychus. Come and help me count the cakes I've baked for supper. |
| *Eutychus* | I'll count everything you want me to count—I love counting. Mother, can we go for a walk tonight and count the goats and the sheep, the tents and the shops, the . . . |
| *Mother* | *(laughing)* Eutychus, Eutychus, not tonight. Paul has come, and we'll all go to church to hear him preach. |
| *Eutychus* | But, Mother, there's nothing to count in church except the minutes till it's over. |
| *Father* | Paul is the great apostle, my son. You may never get to hear him again. He leaves for Jerusalem tomorrow. |
| *Eutychus* | But he preaches so long, and I'm tired. |
| *Father* | Enough of this. Let's go. |

*Family moves to a home church where a group is already listening to Paul's sermon. Mother and Father take places. Eutychus climbs up on a window ledge.*

| | |
|---|---|
| *Eutychus* | *(yawning, to Benjamin, his friend)* Come up here, Benjamin. You can see everything. People look funny from this angle. |
| *Benjamin* | There's not room in the window for two. |
| *Eutychus* | Yes, there is, I'll move over a bit. It's a great place to count. |
| *Benjamin* | I don't want to count. |

| | |
|---|---|
| *Mother* | Hush, children. |

*Benjamin climbs up on ledge next to Eutychus.*

| | |
|---|---|
| *Narrator* | Time passed quickly until Paul's sermon has gone on for hours. |
| *Woman 1* | *(to friend)* I could listen to Paul for hours, couldn't you? |
| *Woman 2* | We have! Why, it's nearly midnight. |
| *Eutychus* | *(to Benjamin)* When is he going to stop? I've never heard anyone talk for so long. I've counted twenty people who have fallen asleep, four flies that have landed on Paul's head, and four children playing chariot races. |
| *Benjamin* | My dad says because Paul may never ever be back, he wants to tell us all he can before he leaves. That's why he's talking so much. |
| *Eutychus* | Why won't he ever come back? |
| *Benjamin* | Because the Jewish leaders hate him and are chasing him down. |
| *Eutychus* | Then I'd better try to stay awake *(head nods)*, but it's . . . it's . . . so har-r-r-d. *(His head rests on his chest as his body slumps and he falls out of the window. There is general panic, and he is declared dead. Paul comes to him, pushing his way through the crowd.)* |
| *Mother* | Paul, Paul, our son is dead! Oh! Oh! |
| *Paul* | Please, Lord, if it be your will, raise this child to life. *(Puts his hand on Eutychus, who revives. The crowd is amazed.)* |
| *Man* | It's a resurrection! As surely as I stand here, he was dead, I mean really dead. Jesus has used Paul to give Eutychus back his life. *(Everyone cheers.)* |
| *Father* | We'd better take Eutychus home and put him to bed. |
| *Eutychus* | *(back on ledge)* No, Father, I want to hear what Paul has to tell me. Now I know this Jesus you all believe in is alive. It is by his power that Paul healed me and I want to count the times he says, "Jesus!" |

*All return to positions.*

| | |
|---|---|
| *Narrator* | Paul continued talking until daybreak. Next time you get bored in church, think of one of the longest sermons that was ever preached. Think of Eutychus and try to stay awake. God may have something *really* important to say to you. Besides, you don't want to fall off your pew and knock yourself out like Eutychus did, do you? |

# Bless the Name

Words and Music by
STUART BRISCOE and LARRY MOORE

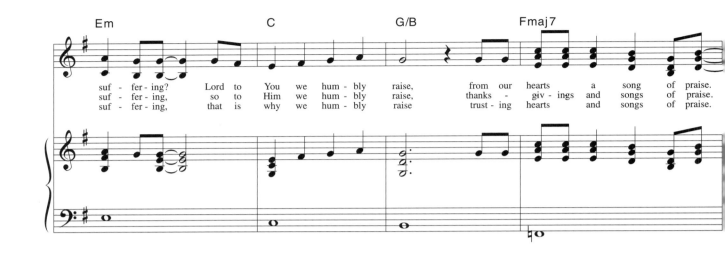

suf - fer - ing? Lord to You we hum - bly raise, from our hearts a song of praise.
suf - fer - ing, so to Him we hum - bly raise, thanks - giv - ings and songs of praise.
suf - fer - ing, that is why we hum - bly raise trust - ing hearts and songs of praise.

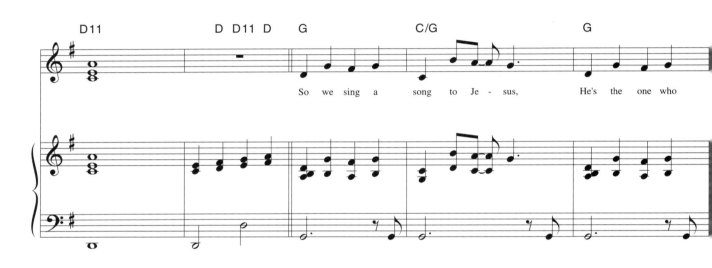

So we sing a song to Je - sus, He's the one who

al - ways sees us, from our care and sor - row frees us, Bless the name of Je - sus

Paul wrote thirteen of the epistles, or letters, in the New Testament. The other epistles were written by different people. James wrote one, Peter wrote two, Jude wrote one, and John wrote three. Then there is the Epistle to the Hebrews. Nobody knows who wrote that, although there have been many guesses.

James was "the Lord's brother," who at first did not believe in Jesus. But after the resurrection he did believe and became a great leader of the church in Jerusalem. His letter sounds like a preacher telling the people what they should do to be good Christians. They should not just say they believe in Jesus but they should show it in the way they live.

Peter wrote his letters to Christians who were having a difficult time because they believed in Jesus. The Jewish priests and priestly rulers did not want people to believe that Jesus was the Son of God and called Christians troublemakers. Christians did not need priests or rulers or pharisees to teach them God's laws because Jesus had given new laws. The Christians had many enemies who wanted to hurt or kill them, especially a wicked emperor in Rome named Nero. Peter told the Christians that they should not be afraid to suffer for Jesus, because Jesus had suffered

# GENERAL EPIST

for them. And they should not forget that Jesus had promised to come again for them one day and that he would be with them until he came back. Soon after Peter wrote these letters he was killed by Nero.

Jude was another brother of Jesus. He was worried about some of the things that were happening in the churches so he wrote a strong letter to show who was causing the problems.

John was the disciple who was very close to the Lord Jesus. John lived to be a very old man and was known to be very loving. He wasn't always like this, because when he was young he was known for his bad temper. But Jesus had changed

John's life. John wanted all Christians to show that they loved the Lord Jesus by loving each other as well.

Hebrews is a letter that explains much of what the Lord Jesus really is. He is far better than anyone or anything else. Only through him can we know God and his salvation. The letter was written for some Jewish people who had become believers but were confused because people said they could not be Jewish and followers of Jesus. This letter showed them that they could be both and that Jesus truly was the Son of God whom the Jewish people had long expected to come to earth.

## TIMOTHY

Timothy lived in Lystra with his mother and grandmother. His father was a Greek and his mother was a Jew. It seems his father had died when Timothy was just a little boy. It's sad when there is no father in the home, but Timothy was happy that he had a wonderful mother and grandmother who had raised him to love the Lord.

Timothy lived in a Christian home. His mother and grandmother believed in Jesus, and from the time Timothy was small he remembered hearing about all the things that Jesus had done before the Romans killed him in Jerusalem. Timothy must have wished he could have met Jesus himself. He knew other boys and girls had been part of a crowd who listened to Jesus. The next best thing, however, was to live in a home where the Scriptures were

taught and the stories of Jesus were repeated over and over again.

Two preachers named Paul and Barnabas came to town one day. There was a crippled man in Lystra who had never walked. Paul preached near the place the crippled man was sitting. The man listened to all that Paul said about Jesus and how he went about doing good and healing people. Paul saw the crippled man look at him and suddenly said to the man, "Stand up on your feet." At that, the crippled man jumped up and began to walk for the first time in his life.

Everyone who was there began to shout. Many of the listeners were Greeks who thought Paul and Barnabas were gods come to earth. (The Greeks believed in many gods.) They gave Barnabas the name Zeus, and they gave Paul the name Hermes. The people began to bring

sacrifices and to worship the two preachers. When Paul and Barnabas realized what was happening, they were horrified.

"We aren't gods," they shouted above all the noise the people were making. "We are men just like you. We've come to tell you about the one true God and his Son Jesus so you can worship him."

All this time some Jews who hated Paul and all Christians talked to the people in the crowd and turned them against Paul and Barnabas.

Timothy, who was just a young boy, was watching all this happen. "Oh, no," he said to his mother, who had brought him to hear Paul preach. "The crowd is angry and have turned against them. Look, they are picking up stones to stone them." Sure enough, they did just that and, thinking Paul was dead, dragged him outside of the city.

The disciples in the crowd gathered around Paul's body. They thought he was dead. Timothy and his mother cried and prayed. Suddenly Paul stirred, got up, and set off back into the city. Christians took him into their home and looked after him and Barnabas. The next morning the two men left for Derbe to continue spreading the gospel.

Timothy couldn't believe all he had seen. He thought Paul was the best preacher he had ever heard. How brave he had been when the people were throwing stones at him. Timothy had a new hero!

Later, when Timothy was older, Paul visited the town again. Paul and Timothy had some good talks about Jesus Christ and about doing his work on earth. Paul began to take Timothy with him on missionary adventures. Timothy was a great helper and soon was preaching and teaching people about Jesus. He became a pastor of a church. Paul and Timothy were almost like father and son. They spent a lot of time together, and Paul sent special news to churches using Timothy as a messenger.

# Let's Pretend

## BEING YOUNG ISN'T EASY

"Greetings, Timothy," called the young woman from the doorway of her modest home. "The sun is shining, the flowers are blooming, the birds are singing. This is the day the Lord has made. The Lord is good!"

"He is indeed," replied Timothy, as he hurried down the steep marble-paved street. "Grace and peace," he added, pushing his way through the busy crowds.

A group of girls who worked at the great temple of Diana passed by. As they saw him, they said, "There goes the preacher boy. Bit young to be a holy man, isn't he?" They laughed and went on their way.

THIS IS A STORY TOLD AS FANTASY MARRIED TO FACT TO BE MIXED WITH FAITH AND LAUGHTER, LOVE AND JOY.

WHAT HAPPENS WHEN A CARTOON BEE CHUG-A-LUGS CARTOON SOAP?

Some men sitting in the shade of a fragrant tree looked up from their game of checkers. "Aren't you going to try to convert us today, preacher boy? Can't handle us, eh? Why don't you send for old Paul to help you out?" One of them spat at Timothy's feet and the others laughed.

*This is the day the Lord has made,* Timothy thought to himself. *I wish he'd made it a little easier. These Ephesians give me a hard time. Even some of the older believers don't listen to me as I try to teach them. "You're too young," they say. "Get a few years under your belt and then you can talk. What do you know about life?"*

By this time he had passed the beautiful library on his left and the great theater on the right. He remembered the terrible scene there when the whole city had rioted against Paul. Timothy had feared for his life. *I hope nothing like that happens again, especially when Paul isn't here,* he thought to himself.

Turning left past the marketplace, he hurried down the long, straight road to the harbor. He was too busy with his thoughts to notice the beautiful pillars and statues of great men who had made Ephesus such an important city. By the time he reached the harbor, the sun was high in the sky and he was quite hot and out of breath. Ships were coming and going, sailors were busy loading and unloading their cargoes. He

watched as a ship with bright white sails came alongside the quay. On the deck a young man was waving excitedly.

"Timothy!" he yelled. "Timothy, it's me, Aristarchus! I have a letter for you from Paul." As his friend ran down the gangway, Timothy rushed to meet him. Timothy was glad to see Aristarchus and to have news from Paul and the rest of the team.

They were so busy talking that Aristarchus forgot to give Timothy the letter. Finally Timothy said, "Aristarchus, would you mind very much if I see Paul's letter now? I can't wait any longer to hear from him. I miss him so much. Never a day goes by when I don't wish a dozen times that he was here with me."

"Sorry," said Aristarchus. "Here, you sit down and read the letter. I'll find my bags."

Eagerly Timothy opened the letter. His eyes skimmed over the neat writing of Paul's assistant to the large messy writing of the great man himself. *His eyesight must be getting worse. His writing is so bad I can hardly read it,* Timothy said to himself. Suddenly his eyes fastened on the words, "Don't let anyone look down on you because you are young."

Timothy put the letter down and looked away, past the busy harbor to where the blue sky and the green ocean met at the horizon. In his imagination he saw the old people in the church who thought he was inexperienced, the men who mocked his attempts to speak to them, the young girls from the temple who laughed at his youthful desire to serve the Lord. "I wish . . ." he started to say aloud.

"You wish what?" Timothy jumped as he heard Aristarchus's question. "You were miles away," said Timothy's friend. "What were you wishing for?"

"Oh, lots of things," sighed Timothy. "I feel so young and the work here is so great and Paul writes that I shouldn't allow people to look down on me because I'm young. But how can I stop them?"

"What else did Paul say?" Aristarchus asked.

Timothy returned to the letter and read aloud, "But set an example for the believers in speech, in life, in love, in faith, and in purity. And if you do, you will save both yourself and your hearers."

"That's it, Timothy! We're young but even young people can live for the Lord because he lives in us. People will see the difference in us and be ready to hear what we have to say. C'mon, Timothy, let's be good examples."

"You're right, Aristarchus. I feel better already. Let's go." Timothy was ready to head back to Ephesus.

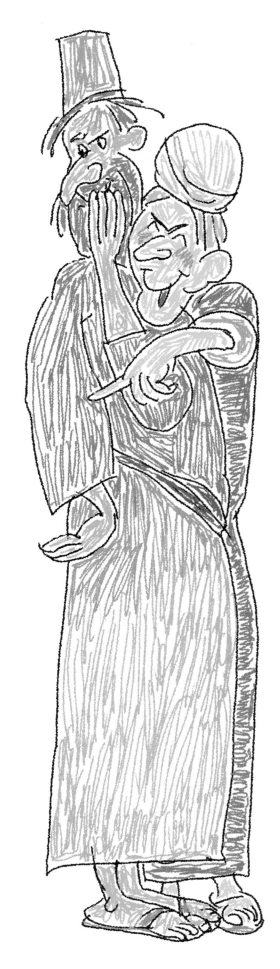

# Timothy & Me

Timothy had tummy trouble all his life. He probably missed a lot of school, couldn't play games, and wasn't very strong. But he never let it stop him from doing what God wanted him to do. That took courage and determination. Who do you think helped Timothy to be brave and strong? Who will help you to serve God even when you think you are too scared or too weak to do much?

# tuff Neat stuff Neat

Schools in Timothy's time were quite different from schools today. Five-year-old boys went to school half-days, six days a week until they were ten years old. When not in school, a boy was learning a trade, usually from his father or perhaps another relative who was a craftsman.

Jewish students really did sit at the feet of their teachers and traced the twenty-two letters of the Hebrew alphabet in the dirt floor or used a stylus on a waxed wooden tablet. After the pupils mastered the alphabet, they learned words and then whole phrases from the Torah (the first five books of the Bible). The Torah was the only "reading" material available. There are no vowels in Hebrew writing so students learned words by memorization and chanted the words to help them learn. It was not considered proper to copy any words from the Torah.

At age ten the boys would go to an advanced class that gave instruction in the Mishnah, a collection of laws added to the Torah. The laws in the Mishnah were told orally (which means by mouth) to generation after generation, and it is often called the "oral" law. The Torah is the "written" law. The Mishnah gave many complicated rules on how to live, how feasts were to be celebrated, how to conduct funerals, and many, many other things.

Not much time was given to physical education, math, music, art, or philosophy in those schools.

Girls were taught by mothers the things they needed to know to be a good wife. They learned how to carry out in their homes the laws boys were learning in school: laws about which foods to eat and how to prepare them, customs and history behind feast days, how to get ready for special holidays, spinning, weaving, how to make medicines from special plants, singing, dancing, and playing an instrument. Only occasionally were girls taught to read.

# Let's Make a Video about

*Your Family Video Theater*

## Timmy's Tummy

PARTICIPANTS ARE ENCOURAGED TO EXPAND AND IMPROVISE,

USING THIS MATERIAL AS A GUIDE. ALLOW YOUR IMAGINATION TO "PEEK AROUND THE CORNER

OF THE VERSE"

AND SEE WHO IS COMING.

AWESOME!

*Cast: Timmy's tummy, heart, eyes, mouth, ears, hands, mind, feet. Note: Characters can form a "body" to act this out.*

| | |
|---|---|
| *Tummy* | Hey, Heart, stop pounding on me. See, you're scared too! It isn't just me! |
| *Heart* | We're all scared! It's scary walking into a town that's so different from the town you were brought up in. And it's scary to try to keep up with Paul. |
| *Tummy* | I wish I could see where we are. Eyes, what can you see up there? |
| *Eyes* | It's so pretty, a little village, the houses in clusters with the river running through the town. |
| *Tummy* | It's not fair being a Tummy. I never get to see all those neat things. |
| *Eyes* | Here we are at the place where the river is wider. Lots of people are selling things. There's a group of women praying. |
| *Mouth* | Here goes! Mind wants me to say something: "I want to tell you all about Jesus of Nazareth whom God sent from heaven to be our Savior." |
| *Tummy* | *(excited)* Timothy must be telling them about Jesus. Oops, here we go again. I'm doing flips. You'd think I was in a circus. |
| *Ears* | Hey, guys. Stop jabbering. I'm trying to hear what's going on. Our Timothy is very busy talking his head off. |
| *Eyes* | *(horrified)* Oh, don't let that happen. If he talks his head off, we'll all be goners. |

| | |
|---|---|
| *Ears* | Listen to this. There are wonderful words coming out of a lady's mouth. Shh—she's saying she believes Jesus died for her. Her name is Lydia. |
| *Eyes* | You should see the gorgeous cloth she's selling. Rich woman too. Should see the way she's dressed. Now Timothy's walking right to the river with her. I hope he doesn't go any further. I can't swim. |
| *Hands* | Careful now, Timothy, hold on to her. |
| *Mouth* | I baptize you in the name of Jesus— |
| *Eyes* | Everyone's running to see what's going on. Oh, oh! look at her face. It's all smiley. |
| *Ears* | Look out! Here come the policemen. They think our guys are troublemakers. |
| *Tummy* | Ow! I've got little pains, like pins and needles all over me. That always happens when we get in trouble with the policemen. |
| *Mind* | Pull yourself together, Tummy; if you're all crunched up with fear poor Timothy won't be able to give you any food to turn into strength to do God's work. |
| *Eyes* | It's okay. They've all gone. Lydia is talking to Paul. She's happy she was baptized. |
| *Ears* | We've all been invited to dinner. Tummy, it's up to you to do your part. Timothy needs to have you behave. Paul needs you to be strong. And Jesus needs you to do your best to keep Timothy healthy. |
| *Feet* | Come along, all of you. We all need a good meal. |
| *Heart* | I'm so happy Lydia and some of her friends became Christians today. |

## 1 Timothy 4:12

"Don't let anyone look down on you because you are young, but set an example for the believers"

# JAMES

Jesus did most of his preaching and teaching when he was with Jewish people. He also was interested in people who were not Jewish. These people were called Gentiles. But Jesus wanted to make sure God's special people heard the gospel first; then they could share it with everybody else. Not all the Jewish people who became followers of Jesus wanted to tell the Gentiles about him, because Jews didn't like Gentiles very much. But God showed Paul and other leaders that they should go and tell everyone about the Lord Jesus.

When Paul and his friends began to do this, they ran into problems. A few of the Jewish people said that the only way people could have their sins forgiven and go to heaven was to keep all the Jewish com-

mandments. By that they meant hundreds of laws that their teachers had put together. Paul said that was not right. People are forgiven when they tell God they are sorry for their sins, thank the Lord Jesus for dying for them, and ask God to forgive them because Jesus died to take away their sins. When they do this, Paul explained, Jesus comes to live in their hearts through the Holy Spirit, who changes them from the inside.

Some of the Jews were unhappy about this teaching and said that Paul was not telling people the truth. So Paul and a few of his friends traveled all the way to Jerusalem to meet with the church leaders. They had a special meeting and there was a big argument. Things could have gotten out of control, but James, the Lord's brother,

was the chairman of the meeting. He was respected by everybody, and when he told the men to be quiet and listen to other people, they did what he said. If James had not been there, the meeting might have ended in a fight.

Certain people at the meeting thought that Christian Gentiles should do everything the Jews did. Peter stood up and said he used to think so too, but God had changed his mind. Peter also made a very good point when he said that the Jews should not tell the Gentiles to do things the way the Jews did them because many of the Jews didn't follow the laws exactly. That made people think.

Then Paul and his friends got up and told many stories about Gentiles who had become disciples of Jesus. They described how their lives had been changed by the Lord and how they were worshiping and serving the Lord just like the people in Jerusalem.

The crowd was divided. Some people thought Paul was right. Others were sure he was wrong. The chairman had to make a decision. What would he say? James listened carefully to everything the people said and then he stood up. Everybody listened as he told them his decision. James said that Paul was right. God had said through the prophets that he would send the Jews to the Gentiles. God had sent Peter to Gentiles, and they had believed. Paul and his friends had many stories of God working in the lives of Gentiles. So the work must go on without the Gentiles being made to do what even the Jews weren't doing.

A few people were not happy with this decision, but they felt better when James said that the Gentiles should respect some of the Jewish laws. Then they all got together and wrote a letter explaining the situation to the people all over the world who had become Christians.

James made a very important decision. His decision has affected even Christians living today. If James had not decided the way he did, Christians today might think that they must become Jews before they could go to heaven. What a good thing it was that James was a wise chairman many years ago.

# Let's Pretend

# HUMPY & DUMPY

Humpy and Dumpy were twins. They were also camels. As they were growing up, the other animals and birds would laugh at them.

Vernon the Vulture flew onto Humpy's floppy hump one day and said, "Look at this silly, floppy thing. What good is Humpy's hump?" Vernon was not very smart, because he should have known that Humpy's hump could hold so much water that Humpy could travel for long distances in the desert where there is no water. That is why camels are called ships of the desert.

Carrie the Cheetah was a fast and beautiful runner. She laughed when she saw Dumpy walk, because Dumpy didn't walk like other animals. She moved both her left legs at the same time and then both her right ones. "Look at that crazy walk," Carrie said. "Why would any animal want to walk like that?" What she didn't know was that camels need to travel for such long distances across wild deserts that they can't worry about graceful speed. They want to make sure they have enough energy to get to the next oasis where they can find food and water.

Wally the Worm almost got trampled one day when Humpy walked by. "Look!" he shouted. "Did you ever see such big, flat feet in all your life? They are the ugliest flattest feet in the whole wide world." Wally should have known that camels have such large, spongy feet because they often have to cross deep sand. Smaller feet would sink in a minute.

Percy the Peacock was very proud. He liked to walk around spreading his blue and green tail. He did it so that he could hear the people say "Ooh" and "Ahh" when he unfolded it in all its long, silky, feathery beauty. Percy thought Humpy's and Dumpy's big knees looked ugly. "Look!" he said. "Look at those big, fat

knees. They look as if they're made for roller blading. I'd like to see a camel on roller blades. At least they won't hurt their knees when they fall. Did you ever see such big, fat, ugly knee pads?" But Percy should have known that camels have such big knees because they spend so much time kneeling down while the loads they must carry across the desert are placed on their backs. Percy was too proud to kneel.

Some of the people who knew the Lord's brother James knew that he had great big pads on his knees just like Humpy and Dumpy. James didn't kneel down so that people could put loads on his back; he knelt down to pray. And he prayed so much that he had knees like a camel. That's why they called him "Camel Knees."

Why would James kneel down to pray? That showed he was not proud before God, that he wanted to humbly confess his sins and ask God to bless him and his work and all the people he worked with.

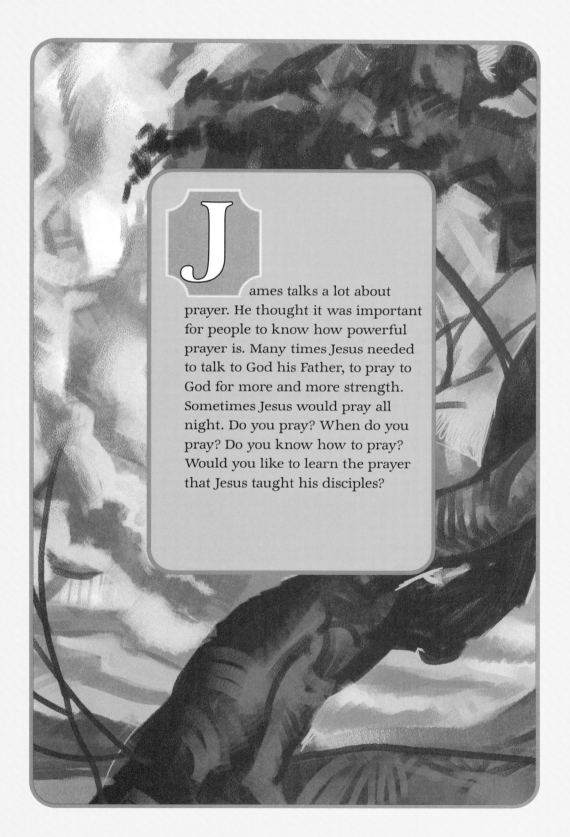

James talks a lot about prayer. He thought it was important for people to know how powerful prayer is. Many times Jesus needed to talk to God his Father, to pray to God for more and more strength. Sometimes Jesus would pray all night. Do you pray? When do you pray? Do you know how to pray? Would you like to learn the prayer that Jesus taught his disciples?

O

ur Father
in heaven,
we honor
your
holy name.

We ask that
your
kingdom
will come
now.

May your will
be done
here on earth,
just as it is
in heaven.

Give us our food
again today,
as usual,

and forgive us
our sins,

just as
we have forgiven
those who have
sinned
against us.

Don't bring us into
temptation,
but deliver us
from the Evil One.

Amen.

Matthew 6:9–13
TLB

# James & Me

The James who wrote the Book of James was one of the brothers of Jesus. Can you imagine what it must have been like having an older brother like Jesus? I would think, wouldn't you, that James would have loved it. Well, the Bible tells us James didn't even believe Jesus was God's son. Once when Jesus was very busy healing and teaching so many people that there wasn't even any time to eat, James and his brothers and Mary, Jesus' mother, came to where he was and tried to make Jesus go home with them. They thought he was crazy.

Maybe you have an older brother who you think is crazy. Sometimes we don't get along as we should with our brothers and sisters. Next time that happens and you feel hurt, remember Jesus went through that too. So because he understands, you can talk to him about it.

After Jesus was raised from the dead, he appeared to James and then James believed in him. James became a leader of the church in Jerusalem, wrote a book that's in the New Testament, and later died for his faith.

# Let's Make a **Video** about

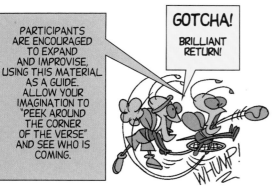

GOTCHA!

BRILLIANT RETURN!

WHUMP!

Your Family Video Theater

**Tommy and Tammy**

*James*

*Cast: Tammy, Tommy*

*Scene: A room in their house.*

*Tammy walks into the room to find her twin brother, Tommy, sticking his fingers into his mouth. She wonders what he is trying to do.*

| | |
|---|---|
| *Tammy* | Tommy, what are you doing? Did you swallow something? |
| *Tommy* | *(taking his hand out of his mouth)* I'm trying to get ahold of my tongue, but it's very hard. It's too slippery. |
| *Tammy* | Yuk! You're gross. Why would anyone want to get ahold of their tongue? |
| *Tommy* | Because Mother told me to. |
| *Tammy* | Are you telling me that Mother told you to stick your hand in your mouth and try to pull out your tongue? |
| *Tommy* | No, she just said, "Tommy, hold your tongue!" |
| *Tammy* | *(laughing)* Tommy, you're weird. She didn't mean that you should hold your tongue, she meant, "Hold your tongue." |
| *Tommy* | Well, what's the difference? She said, "Hold your tongue." That's what I'm trying to do. |
| *Tammy* | Well, it's like when Mother told you, "Wipe your feet" when you came into the house with muddy shoes. She didn't mean that you had to wipe your feet. She meant, "Wipe your shoes." |
| *Tommy* | So, why don't grown-ups say what they mean? |
| *Tammy* | She means that you should stop saying what you are saying. |

| *Tommy* | Oh! I see. So it's like when I hold the dog to keep it from running away. I should hold my tongue because sometimes it runs away on me and I say things I shouldn't say. |
| --- | --- |
| *Tammy* | What did you say to Mother? |
| *Tommy* | *(teasing)* I can't tell you! I have to hold my tongue! |
| *Tammy* | *(after a long pause)* Go on, say something. You can't hold your tongue forever. |
| *Tommy* | I was using the quiet to do a little thinking. Maybe holding my tongue and thinking instead is not such a bad idea after all. |
| *Tammy* | What were you thinking? |
| *Tommy* | Girls always want to know what you're thinking. |
| *Tammy* | Watch your tongue, young man! |

*Tommy, laughing, runs over to the mirror and sticks out his tongue.*

| *Tammy* | What are you doing now? |
| --- | --- |
| *Tommy* | What you told me to do. I'm watching my tongue. |
| *Tammy* | You are silly. |
| *Tommy* | *(joking)* Now it's your turn to hold your tongue. |
| *Tammy* | When I say "Watch your tongue" it's the same as when Daddy said to you "Watch your head" when you ducked under the stairs looking for a ball. |
| *Tommy* | *(laughing)* Yes, it's hard to watch your head without taking your eyes out, isn't it? |
| *Tammy* | So "Watch your tongue" means to be careful of what you are saying. |
| *Tommy* | And "Hold your tongue" means to stop saying bad things. |
| *Tammy* | I know what we should do. Let's play a game. Let's think of good things to do with our tongues. You go first. |
| *Tommy* | Lick an ice cream cone. |
| *Tammy* | No, silly . . . |
| *Tommy* | Ah, ah! |
| *Tammy* | Sorry. I wasn't watching my tongue. |
| *Tommy* | Okay, I'll try again. Let me think. I know. I'll say something nice. That would be a good thing to do with my tongue. |

| | |
|---|---|
| *Tammy* | Go on then, say something nice to me. |
| *Tommy* | Er, er, I know! You are my favorite sister. |
| *Tammy* | That wasn't exactly nice. I'm your only sister. |
| *Tommy* | But you're still my favorite. |
| *Tammy* | In that case, what you said was true. |
| *Tommy* | And it was kind. |
| *Tammy* | Are you sure? |
| *Tommy* | Oh, yes! I used my tongue to say something true and kind. |
| *Tammy* | Good. That's what tongues are for. |

The tongue is a small thing, but what enormous damage it can do. James 3:5 TLB

The last book in the Bible is called Revelation. It was written by John, the disciple whom Jesus loved very much. John continued to live a long time after Jesus went back to heaven. As an old man he was one of the leaders of the church in Ephesus. But certain people who did not like him had him sent far away from his home to live on a little island called Patmos.

One morning John had a vision—a special kind of dream. In the vision he saw all kinds of strange and wonderful things about the Lord Jesus. Some of the things he saw were so wonderful he could hardly describe them. John tried to write down what angels look like and what heaven is like. Because it was hard for him to find proper words to explain such wonderful things, the Book of Revelation is sometimes hard for us to understand. In the vision John learned many things about the Lord that he had not known before. It was as if God opened John's eyes so he could understand things he had never understood. That is what revelation means.

The vision showed John that it would be very hard for some people to be Christians. John knew that already. It was hard for him to be so far away from home. But the good news for John was that the Lord Jesus would be the winner in the end. In the vision John saw many strange things that helped him understand why there was so much evil and suffering in the world. But through it all he saw that the Lord Jesus was still in charge.

# THE BOOK OF REVEL

When we watch TV we see things that have happened in the past. Sometimes we watch something while it happens, like a ball game. But in John's vision God allowed him to see things before they happened. This was helpful to John. When he was sad because he was away from his family and friends, he remembered that Jesus would make sure everything worked out fine in the end.

In the vision John was told to write down the things he saw. He could then send a letter to his friends in the church at Ephesus and share with them the good news about what God was doing and would do in the world. The people were so happy to receive John's letter, or Revelation, that they saved it. Later it was put in the Bible, and now we can read it long after John wrote it. We, too, can learn about what God is doing and is going to do.

ATION

# JOHN'S VISION

The old man with long, gray hair slowly made his way up the hill. He paused to catch his breath, leaning heavily on his staff. The sun glinted on the bright blue-green water of the harbor. A small boat with red sails cut through the small, choppy waves. The old man's eyes followed the boat's course for a number of minutes. Then he turned and with a sigh began to climb again. "That boat will be in Ephesus in a day or two, Lord. That's where I'd love to go too. Is there no way you can get me off this island and back to my friends in the church there?"

The path led into an opening in the flowering bushes. There sat a group of men and women with a few children. As the old man walked into the group, they all rose and said, "The Lord be with you, John."

He replied, "And with your spirit."

A man began to sing a psalm very quietly, and the other people joined in. John's voice was surprisingly strong for such an old man. An old woman stood to pray, and as she talked to the Lord some of the people began to weep quietly. When she had finished, John began to speak.

"Brothers and sisters," John said, "we must love each other." John went on to talk about the days he had walked the streets of Palestine with Jesus, how Jesus had healed the sick and forgiven people's sins. Then with tears in his eyes, John talked about how much Jesus had loved everybody—enough to die on the cross. John told the small group about the way he and the other disciples had run away from the Lord. John's voice broke, and for a minute he was not able to talk. Then John looked up, and a great smile crossed his face.

93

"But," John said, "on the first day of the week Jesus rose again. And here we are to remember him as he told us to." With that John took a small loaf of bread and a small flask of wine, prayed over them, and handed them to the group. Quietly they ate and drank, remembering the Lord's broken body and shed blood.

The heat of the day, the long climb up the hill, and the effort of speaking seemed too much for old John. He sat down heavily and seemed to drift into a peaceful sleep. The group closed their meeting and quietly walked away to their homes, leaving a young woman to watch over John. As she watched the old man, she knew he must be dreaming. Suddenly his head jerked up and he turned around as if he had heard a loud noise. She didn't know it, but John had heard the sound of a great trumpet. His face immediately began to glow like the sun, and a smile like one she had never seen lit up his face. John was seeing the risen Lord himself.

The old man dropped to his knees and raised his hands as if to catch hold of someone. Quietly he began to move his lips. The young woman leaned closer to hear what he was saying. "Yes, Master. I will hear what you have to say, and I will write it down and send a letter to the churches."

The young woman watched old John's face. The smile faded and tears began to flow down his sunburned cheeks. Then a look of horror passed like a shadow across his face. *What is he seeing?* she wondered.

John looked at her and said, "Quickly, child, bring me a pen and some scrolls." He started writing fast. She watched while he filled up first one, then two, then seven scrolls. She had no idea how long she stayed there and waited quietly. Suddenly John's eyes opened. He stood up with some difficulty as she helped him.

"Are you all right, John?" she asked.

John looked at her as if surprised to see her and then said, "Child, I have seen unbelievable things. I had to find earthly words to write about these heavenly things. Some of the glorious things God has shown me can't be talked about on earth. We'll have to wait until we get to heaven to understand how beautiful it is there."

For a long time John talked about the strange and wonderful things he had seen. When he had finished, he looked at her and said, "Thanks be unto God."

"Amen," she said quietly, as she helped him pick up the scrolls.

John had written special letters to seven churches. Later those letters became part of the Book of Revelation, which would be read all over the world by people who want to know what God is doing and will do in the world.

# Let's Pretend

## THE LION AND THE LAMB

THIS IS A STORY TOLD AS FANTASY MARRIED TO FACT TO BE...MIXED WITH...FAITH AND...AND LAUGHTER, LOVE...AND AND AND AND AND **JOY.**

COME ON, YOU CAN DO IT. **YOU'RE ALMOST DONE!!!**

Tommy and Tammy's mother called from the bottom of the stairs, "Are the children ready, dear?" Her husband called back, "Almost. They've had their showers and they're putting on their pajamas. We won't be a minute."

Mother hummed happily as she made the children their favorite bedtime drinks and snacks. "We've had a great day," she said to herself. She liked to talk to herself when she was alone. "Yes, a great day," she added, though nobody was there to hear.

The children came running down the stairs and bounced into the den. "Here are your drinks," said Mother. They curled up on the sofa in front of the fire and started to make their snacks disappear. "Not so fast," Mother said. "You'll gobble your food so quickly that you will have a

tummyache." The children laughed and said they wouldn't. But Mother knew they would.

Just then Dad came into the room, drying his hands. "That bathroom looked as if a tornado had hit it," he said to the children, who knew what he meant. They looked into the bottom of their mugs and smiled quietly at each other. "When I was a boy . . ." he started to say.

"Yes, dear," said his wife, "what happened when you were a boy?"

"Never mind," he said, realizing that his children and his wife were smiling because he often told them how different life was when he was a boy. "Let's talk about our day," he said, changing the subject quickly.

"It was a great day," said Mother. Turning to the children, she asked, "What did you like best about our day at the zoo?"

"The lion," shouted Tommy.

"The lamb," said Tammy.

"The lion was best," shouted Tommy. "Only sissy girls like lambs."

"The lamb was better than the lion," said Tammy. "It was warm and curly, and I could pet it. Only nasty boys like lions."

"Now, children," said Mother, "we've had a great day. Let's not spoil it now."

JOHN the BAPTIST

95

"Well, lions are big and strong. They look fierce, and I like the way their yellow eyes look at you without blinking," said Tommy. "I don't think they're afraid of anything."

"They are called the king of beasts, you know, Tommy," said his dad.

"Well, I still like lambs better. They're gentle and playful. You couldn't play with a lion. It would get angry with you. And lambs have such pretty eyes. They look as if they want you to be their friend," insisted Tammy.

"You two don't have to agree on one animal. It's okay to have different favorites. Let me ask you a question," said Dad. "Do you think it would be possible to get a lamb that is like a lion or a lion that is like a lamb?"

"That's silly. How could a lion be like a lamb? It would open its great big mouth and out would come a little bleat," said Tommy. "That would be one confused lion."

"Or the lamb would open its mouth and roar like a lion," said Tammy. "That would scare everybody, including the lamb."

"Well, let me tell you two something. The Bible talks about a lion that looked like a lamb," said Dad.

"Where does it say that?" the twins shouted at the same time.

"I'll get a Bible," said Tammy.

"Let's see," said Dad, "the story I'm looking for is in the Book of Revelation. Here it is. In his vision John saw the Lord sitting on his throne holding a scroll. An important angel shouted with a loud voice, 'Who is worthy to open the scroll?' Nobody came forward. John was so sorry about this because he wanted to know what was written in the scroll. Then an elder told John to stop weeping because the Lion of the Tribe of Judah could open the scroll. John turned to see the lion and couldn't believe his eyes. The lion was a lamb—a very special lamb. Obviously it had been killed, but it was standing up!"

Tammy shuddered when she heard that. "I don't think I like this lamb," she said.

But Tommy shouted, "I think this is cool. Go on, Dad!"

Dad began to explain. "It's like this. What John saw was a vision of the Lord Jesus that was so wonderful there were no ordinary words to explain it. So he used a word picture, or symbol. When John said Jesus was the lion, what do you think he meant, Tommy?"

"He meant that Jesus is strong and brave like a lion, I guess," Tommy replied.

"Right. And when John said that Jesus was like a lamb, what do you think that meant, Tammy?"

"That he is gentle and kind?"

"Right. Jesus is both strong and kind, brave and gentle," Mother said.

"But why did he say that the lamb was standing up after it was dead?" asked Tommy.

"I know," said Tammy, jumping up and down and holding up her hand as if she were in school. "It was because Jesus died on the cross and then he rose again."

"Yeah, that's right," said Tommy. "That's neat."

"But there's one thing we shouldn't forget," added Mother. "Jesus was the 'Lamb of God who takes away the sin of the world.'"

"And he will reign as the King of kings forever," said Dad.

"Like a lion," shouted Tommy. "I still like lions best."

"Well, I like lambs best," Tammy replied.

"That's enough, you two," said Dad. "You can have your favorite animals if you wish. Remember that Jesus is the lion who looked like a lamb."

"The lamb who took away the sin of the world," said Tammy.

"The lion who will reign as King of kings," said Tommy.

"Bedtime!" said Mother, who knew the discussion could go on longer if it delayed bedtime

The way she said it made both Tommy and Tammy get up and head for the stairs. On the way up Tommy tried a little roar.

# John & Me

    Can you imagine what it would be like to try to explain colors to a blind person? How would you do it? Maybe you would say red is "hot" like fire because you know a blind person can "feel" heat even though he or she can't see the flames. Saying *hot* wouldn't be like actually seeing red, would it? You would know that the only way a blind person could really understand would be to get sight back.

    When John tried to tell us what heaven was like (God let him have a look, remember?) it was very hard, like describing colors to a blind person. We will only really "see" what John saw when we get there ourselves. Anyway, John did the very best that he could do.

    One day we will see all the wonderful things and people in heaven for ourselves if we ask Jesus Christ to forgive us for our sins and be our Savior and friend.

**New things we'll have in heaven:**

new bodies, new language, new places to live, new names, new clothes, new food.

## Things we'll never see in heaven:

first-aid stations, hospitals, crutches, wheelchairs, cars, airplanes, trains, boats, night, computers, televisions, schools, police officers, fire departments, jails.

## Things we'll never be in heaven:

bored, sick, mean, hungry, thirsty, hurting, afraid, lonely, sad, late, worried.

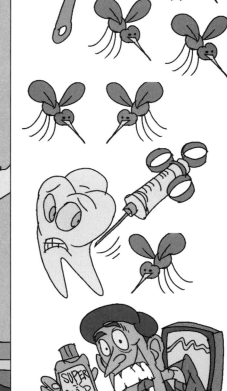

# Let's Make a **Video** about

PARTICIPANTS ARE EN- EN- ENCOURAGED TO EX-EX-PAND AND IMP-IMPROVISE, USING THIS MATERIAL AS A G-G-G-G-G- GUIDE........

........ALLOW YOUR IMAGINATION TO.......

........."PEEK AROUND THE CORNER......

......OF THE VERSE" AND SEE WHO IS.....

......COMING.

IT'S OVER!

IT'S OVER! IT'S OVER! IT'S OVER!

Your Family Video Theater

## Singers

*Cast: Doe, Ray*

| | |
|---|---|
| *Narrator* | There is a break in a choir rehearsal in heaven, and two choir members, Doe and Ray, are talking together. |
| *Doe* | Hi. What's your name? |
| *Ray* | My name's Ray. What's yours? |
| *Doe* | Dothan, but my friends call me Doe. Call me Doe. I guess we're all friends here, aren't we? |
| *Ray* | Right. Marvelous place, isn't it? I had no idea what to expect. But this is fantastic. I'd read a little of the book in the Bible called *Revelation,* but I never really understood it. It kind of described heaven, but I had the feeling there were a lot of heavenly things that people on earth couldn't imagine. |
| *Doe* | What d'you mean? |
| *Ray* | Well, take the music up here. I'd read about us all playing harps. |
| *Doe* | *(laughing)* And you weren't into harps, right? |
| *Ray* | Are you kidding me! An electric guitar was as close as I ever got to a harp. And I had the idea that we would wear white robes and sprout wings. And look at us. No wings. Not even feathers. |
| *Doe* | Yeah, but look how we can get around. We can be here one second, and not here but there the next second. Well, we talk about seconds, but there are no seconds in heaven because there is no time in heaven. But you get the idea. |

102

| | |
|---|---|
| *Narrator* | Just for fun Doe and Ray went from where they were to where they weren't, which was the other side of the universe, and were back in a flash. (You must not try to do this while you are on earth because, until you get to heaven, you'll have to be content staying where you are unless you fly by jet. And even the fastest jet is turtle-slow compared with travel in heaven.) When Doe and Ray got back, they continued their conversation. |
| *Ray* | How did you get here? |
| *Doe* | How did I get where? Heaven, you mean? |
| *Ray* | Right. I mean, did you die some time ago, or did you come when the Lord returned to earth for his people? |
| *Doe* | Oh, I died when I was very young. Chariot wreck. |
| *Ray* | Chariot? You've got to be kidding. What year was it? |
| *Doe* | Well, it was in the Year of Our Lord 99. |
| *Ray* | Is that the same as A.D. 99? |
| *Doe* | You got it. A.D. 99. |
| *Ray* | Well, how did it happen? The chariot wreck, I mean. |
| *Doe* | We were in the games in Rome. Going at a tremendous speed—for those days, you understand. We got tangled up with another chariot and our horses crashed to the ground and I was thrown out on to the arena floor and another chariot ran over me. The last thing I heard was the scream of the crowd. They loved it. Then the next thing I knew I was here and everything was wonderful. |
| *Ray* | What was it like waiting? All that time! Hundreds of years have passed since your chariot wreck. What have you been doing? |
| *Doe* | What strange questions you ask. There's no time here, remember? It's just as if everything is right now. |
| *Ray* | Takes some getting used to, doesn't it? May I ask you something else? |
| *Doe* | Sure. |
| *Ray* | If you lived in Rome, you must have spoken Latin. Where did you learn such good English? |

| | |
|---|---|
| *Doe* | *(laughing)* You must be an American or an Englishman. Your kind think we speak English in heaven. I'm not speaking English. |
| *Ray* | You must be, because I don't understand Latin. |
| *Doe* | And I never learned English, because your kind of English wasn't invented when I was alive. |
| *Ray* | Well, what's going on? How come we understand each other? |
| *Doe* | This is heaven, remember? We speak and hear and understand in the language of heaven. It is all part of the new system. But tell me, when did you arrive? Were you killed too? Did you die like an old man? Or were you on earth when the Master came for you? |
| *Ray* | I didn't die. I was busy living my life, serving the Lord, and he came. I'd been expecting him but in a way I really didn't expect him. |
| *Doe* | Well, he told us to be ready, didn't he? |
| *Ray* | Yes, and I was—but in a way I wasn't. |
| *Doe* | Well, what happened? |
| *Ray* | This is going to sound strange to you, but I—er—I don't really know what happened. It was so sudden. |
| *Doe* | In the twinkling of an eye, eh? |
| *Ray* | Right. It was that quick. It was sort of—whoosh—and we were here! |
| *Doe* | Sounds exciting. Much better than being killed. |
| *Doe* | Well, here come some more choir members. D'you like singing? |
| *Ray* | I do now. I didn't down there. |
| *Doe* | I've always loved singing, but I didn't have the voice. |
| *Ray* | Strange, isn't it? I didn't like singing and now I love it. You couldn't sing and now you sing like an angel. |
| *Doe* | I guess that's what heaven is like. We're all changed—for the better. |
| *Ray* | Amen. It amazes me to think that the Lord who invented music would want to hear us sing. |
| *Doe* | Yes, but how can we not sing when we see the Savior? |

*Narrator*    And now listen to the song they sang. It's called "Now's the Time to Sing." By the way, I said at the beginning that there was a break in the action. But there could not be a break because that would take time and there's no time in heaven. So if you're confused, don't worry. So am I. But we'll all understand heaven when we get there. We can look for Doe and Ray. And I'll be looking for you.

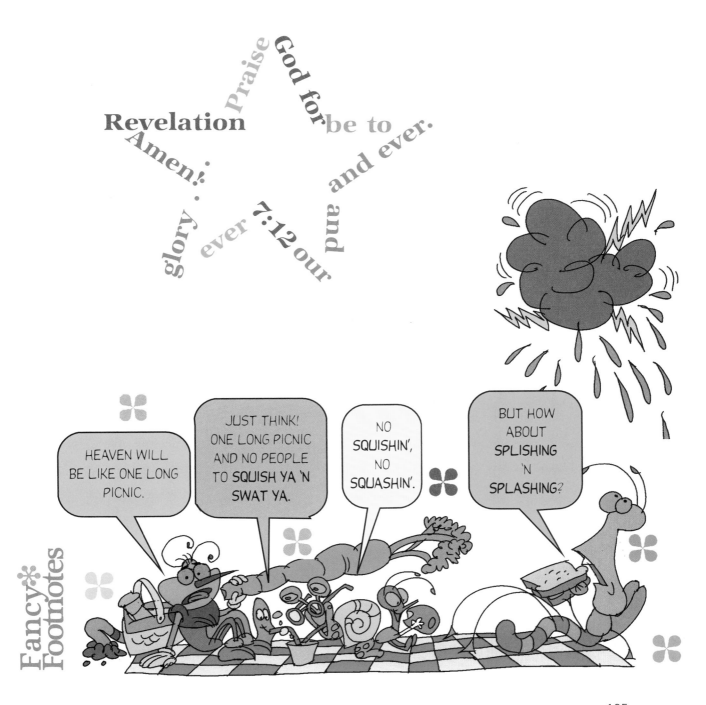

# Now's the Time to Sing

Words and Music by
STUART BRISCOE and LARRY MOORE

We hope you've met such friends in these books
That you'll return to have second looks.
Abram, Noah, Daniel and his den
Can always be visited again.

At bedtime, midday, or in the morning hour
Let these new friendships bud and grow and flower.
May Peter, Paul, and Mary's stories tell
You how to really know God well.

And may we, writers, readers, artists too,
And publishers who have made this book for you
Be found around God's throne in endless ages
With those we've learned to love within these pages!

These innovative books will appeal to parents who want to teach biblical truths to their children in a fresh and exciting way. The interactive presentation of Bible stories, using songs, drama, and cartoons, makes the **B.I.B.L.E.** books ideal for family devotions. Kids will actually look forward to spending time together learning about God's word. No more coaxing and cajoling.

This multi-media approach can add excitement and enrichment to other educational settings:

- Home school
- Christian school
- Children's church
- Sunday school

Songs and readings from these books are also available on audio.

Six adventures are waiting in each book of the **B.I.B.L.E.** series. Take an excursion with your family from creation through the New Testament. Look below at characters and events found in all four books:

$14.99 each • Hardback • 112 pages

## Moses Takes a Road Trip
### And Other Famous Journeys

- *Creation*
- *Adam and Eve*
- *Noah*
- *Abram*
- *Moses*
- *Joshua*

ISBN 0-8010-4183-X

## Jesus Makes a Major Comeback
### And Other Amazing Feats

- *John the Baptist*
- *Jesus' Birth*
- *Jesus' Miracles*
- *Jesus' Big Week*
- *Jesus' Resurrection*
- *Luke*

ISBN 0-8010-4197-X

## David Drops a Giant Problem
### And Other Fearless Heroes

- *Samuel*
- *David*
- *Solomon*
- *Jeremiah*
- *Daniel*
- *Jonah*

ISBN 0-8010-4216-X

## Paul Hits the Beach
### And Other Wild Adventures

- *Peter*
- *Paul's Life*
- *Paul's Journeys*
- *Timothy*
- *James*
- *John*

ISBN 0-8010-4202-X

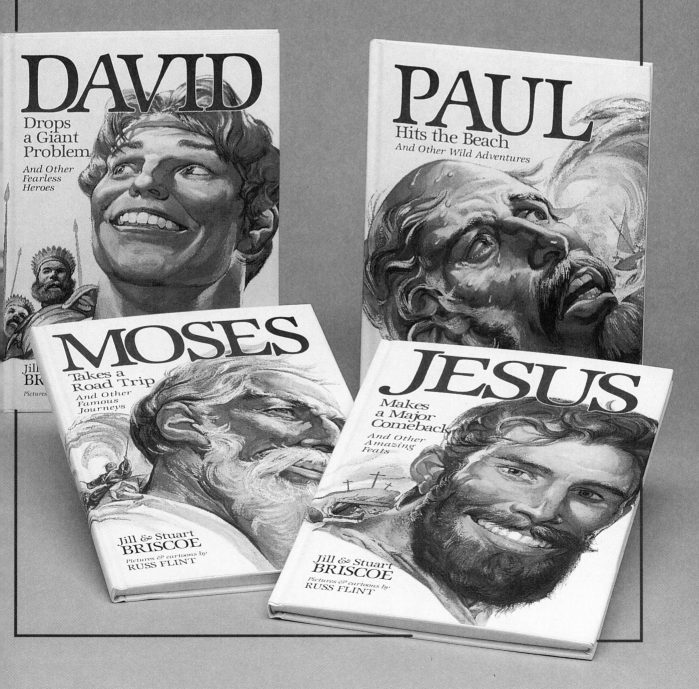

# BAKER INTERACTIVE BOOKS FOR *Lively* EDUCATION

**DAVID** Drops a Giant Problem
And Other Fearless Heroes

**PAUL** Hits the Beach
And Other Wild Adventures

**MOSES** Takes a Road Trip
And Other Famous Journeys

Jill & Stuart BRISCOE
Pictures &

**JESUS** Makes a Major Comeback
And Other Amazing Feats

Jill & Stuart BRISCOE
Pictures & cartoons by
RUSS FLINT

**Jill** and **Stuart Briscoe** are the parents of three grown children and the grandparents of nine. Jill has written more than forty books, and Stuart more than fifty. Stuart serves as senior pastor of Elmbrook Church in Brookfield, Wisconsin. Jill is an advisor to women's ministries at the church, and director of Telling the Truth media and ministries. Both are worldwide speakers at retreats and conferences. The Briscoes live in Oconomowoc, Wisconsin.

**Russ Flint** is the designer/illustrator of many children's books, including *Let's Make a Memory, Let's Hide a Word, My Very First Bible,* and *Teach Me About Jesus.* He regularly contributes artwork to such magazines as *Ideals* and *Guideposts for Kids* and is cofounder of Dayspring Card Company. He has also illustrated such familiar classics as *Legend of Sleepy Hollow, A Christmas Carol, Swan Lake,* and *Little Women.* He lives in Greenville, California.

If I could meet Paul I would like to ask him:

What are the most important Christian rules?

What is the kindest thing I can do for someone?